White Rabbit

Lucky LeFou

Table of Contents

Prequel

7

Part 1

77

Part 2

123

Prequel

Preface

Sighing, Nathan ran his hand through his short black hair as he hesitantly made his way to the automatic doors of the hospital entrance. Anxiety pulsed through his body like lightning. He always hated starting blood transfusions at new facilities. After checking in, he took a seat in the waiting room. It didn't take long before he could feel the haunting stares of the room's other occupants. It's not common to see a man with a green-tinted complexion.

"Nathan?" a younger, bright, blue-eyed nurse called. Her eyes reminded him of sapphires as they reflected the fluorescent lights above. Carefully, he stood and walked over to her. "Good morning. I'm Ivy; I'll be your nurse today." She beamed, gesturing for him to follow her. A few nurses turned and watched as they passed the nurse's station and to the treatment room. Nathan sat in the chair as the nurse pulled the curtain closed in the doorway, "This isn't your first transfusion, correct?"

Nathan shook his head, "No. I've been getting them for a few years now. I'm just new to this facility." Reclining the chair, Ivy began charting his vitals. He fought to control his breathing as he looked at the ceiling tiles above him. Every transfusion brought a new set of questions and scenarios flooding his mind. "I'm very sorry, could you bring me a blanket? I tend to get cold during the transfusions." He asked, watching as she made her way over to him and began to clean the area with an alcohol wipe.

Without eye contact, Ivy hung the saline and medication bags to the IV pole beside Nathan, "Absolutely. Let me start the saline flush, and I will grab you one from the warmer." After verifying that the clamps were open and the saline was flowing properly, she slipped out of the room. As quickly as she left, she returned with the blanket and laid it on Nathan.

"That was fast. You're as swift as a rabbit." He chuckled, causing Ivy to blush. "Nurses have to be quick. I'm going to switch you over now. I will stay with you for the first bit to keep an eye out for any adverse reactions and to make sure you don't need anything. "She smiled, pushing a chair over next to him.

Nathan pulled the blanket closer to his face, realizing he felt oddly comfortable. He wasn't sure if it was the soft, brilliant blue eyes watching over him or his overall sense of safety in the new location. Overcome by the warmth of the blanket, Nathan fell asleep.

The cracking sound of the billiard balls accompanied the laughter and chatter of the bar. Nathan swirled the contents of his glass as he leaned against the counter. He had never been a fan of crowded spaces, but he couldn't say no this time. It was his best friend's bachelor party, and unlike most parties, he decided to have it at the bar and not the strip club.

A hand gently brushed down the length of his spine, causing him to sit up straight. "Now, Nathan, I know you aren't sitting here drinking," a voice teased. He recognized the voice and smiled, "Well, if it isn't a wild rabbit. I know better; it's just soda, darling." He turned to face Ivy, who was now standing at his side and smiling. Her silky black dress caused her features to stand out more. Instantly, he began to blush, "You look gorgeous, but you also seem a bit overdressed for a venue such as this." Ivy leaned on the counter and shrugged. "It's Katie's birthday, so we went to dinner, and then she decided she wanted to come here. I'm not a fan of places like this, but I wasn't going to say no."

Nathan gulped down the rest of his drink as the pair watched Katie do a few rounds of shots that various men lined up to buy her. Katie reminded Nathan of a caterpillar, but he would never tell her that. Ivy had been away on vacation for his last few blood transfusions, and Katie had filled in for her. She was nice enough, but she wasn't Ivy in the least. Clearing his throat, he gently placed his hand on her forearm. Smiling, she looked back at him.

"Rabbit, I was wondering. I've wanted to ask you for a while now, but transfusions didn't seem like the best time to ask. Could I take you to dinner one night?"

Her eyes widened at his question. "There are a lot of factors that come into play. I do like you, Nathan, but I need to figure some things out first. How about I give you an answer at your appointment next week?" she giggled nervously, playing with her hair. Katie had yelled something from across the bar that seemed like she was calling Ivy over, but it was so slurred that she couldn't be sure. Nathan smiled and nodded at her. She smiled, turned, and made her way towards where Katie was dancing.

His heart felt as if it had been ripped from his chest as he watched her walk away. She didn't say no, but finding the nerve to ask such a question was no easy task for a man with a condition like his. He hadn't told her about how his health had started to decline while she was away; he didn't want to worry her. Reaching beneath the bar, he pulled out his cane that he had hidden. Slowly, he made his way over to the rest of the bachelor party, congratulated his friend, and headed home.

Ivy began preparing the treatment room for Nathan's arrival. She hadn't spoken to him since the night at the bar but was ecstatic to see him today. Deciding it was for the best, she didn't bother to mention their conversation to Katie or anyone else.

After arranging everything on the counter, her chair placed next to his, and a warm blanket waiting, she made her way to the waiting room. Opening the door, her smile faded. He wasn't there. Glancing at the clock, she noticed it was five minutes after his appointment. Nathan was never late, nor did he miss his appointments.

Quickly, she returned to the nurse's station, "Hey, has anyone heard from Nathan? He isn't here." The nurses shrugged or shook their heads in response. Her heart began to race as she pulled out her phone and called him.

"Hello?" Nathan mumbled

"H-hey! I wanted to check with you. It's time for your appointment, and I didn't see you in the waiting room."

"I-I," Nathan cleared his throat, "I'm here, but I cannot leave my car. I'm so sorry, I tried."

"Wait, let me come to you. Are you parked in your usual spot?"

"Yes."

"Hang tight, I'm on my way."

Ivy hung up the phone and snatched the warm blanket from the treatment chair. Heading to the door, she tossed the blanket on the wheelchair and pushed it out the door. She swiftly made her way across the parking lot and over to Nathan's car. The car was still running, and Nathan rested his head against the headrest with his eyes closed.

Carefully opening the door, she reached in, turned the car off, and slid the car key into her scrub pocket. He slowly opened his eyes, allowing the tears he held back to flow quietly down his face. "I'm sorry," he whispered, barely loud enough for her to hear. She gently wiped the tears from his face and smiled softly, "Hey, you're okay. I'm going to get you inside, and we'll see what's going on."

Nathan did the best he could to assist Ivy with placing him in the wheelchair. Once he was seated securely, she wrapped the warm blanket around him and made her way back inside. Pressing the button on the pager located near the neck of her scrubs, she informed Katie and the other nurses that she was assisting Nathan to the emergency department and to page her if she was needed. He gently laid his head against her arm as she wheeled him through the double doors and to the reception counter to check him in.

The staff wasted no time getting him into a room because of the severity of his case and past medical history. Ivy assisted the staff in moving the frail man from the chair to the bed, taking his vitals, and updating his chart. Nathan did the best he could to answer the questions asked before he passed out from the pain.

It didn't take long before they started drawing blood and running the tests the staff felt were necessary. Once the results were back, the doctor entered the room scratching his head, "Ivy, his tests are normal."

"There's no way. There is something seriously wrong. There's absolutely no way the tests are normal. You're focusing on his liver, right?"

"Liver? Why would I focus on his liver?"

"He's green. Just based on appearance alone, you should have been able to notice he has high biliverdin levels, and if you read his chart at all, you would have seen he's had a liver transplant and is receiving blood transfusions."

The doctor started thumbing through Nathan's chart and wandered out the door. Ivy sighed heavily, pinching the bridge of her nose as she moved a chair closer to his bed. Sitting down, she gently took his hand and glanced at the monitors. Thankfully, she called him. They would have transported him and ultimately decided to send him home based on the supposed normal results from his blood work.

More staff members made their way into the room and took Nathan for additional testing over the course of a few hours. She closely watched his vitals and started making her own notes. His eyes fluttered open, and he slowly began to look around. She moved in closer and brushed some stray strands of hair from his face, "Your hair is getting long." He smiled weakly, "I haven't been able to do much lately. I haven't been well for a few weeks now."

"Are you warm enough? I can get you another blanket if you would like."

"No, sweet rabbit, I'm okay. Just stay here with me."

She sat back in the chair, still holding his hand, and scooted in closer. Carefully, she rested her head on his shoulder, "So, where are we going for dinner when you feel better?" He chuckled softly, "Anywhere you want. You decide, and I'll make it happen." As the doctor returned, she gently rubbed the back of his hand with her thumb. "You were right. I didn't pay attention, and I apologize. The results from the last set of tests are in, and unfortunately, his body is rejecting the liver. He's been added to the list again, and we are changing up his medication to see if we can at least get him comfortable while we wait. If we can get things to balance out a bit, we will send him home until another liver is available."

The doctor took his leave as tears silently dripped onto Nathan's shoulder. "Oh no, sweet rabbit. It's okay. I've been here before. I have you by my side this time, so I have a much better chance."

"I'm not going anywhere. I'm taking notes so we can use them as a reference in the future. I'll do what I can to stay on top of your treatments and medications, I promise."

3

Nathan sat at the bar of the restaurant, casually sipping water while waiting for Ivy. Two twin men across the bar caught his attention. They both had spiked dirty blond hair, button-up shirts, khaki shorts, and sandals. Usually, he wouldn't have paid attention to what they were wearing, but it was November and quite chilly. The twins locked eyes with Nathan, who shyly looked away. A few moments later, they made their way to him and stood one on each side.

"Hey, bro, you seem like you're having a rough time," one remarked, giving Nathan a bump on the shoulder. "Yeah, bro, rough time. We can help with that," the second said, nodding at his brother. He cleared his throat, not daring to look at either of them, "No, I'm okay, thanks."

"Nah, we know a way to get that pain to go away."

"Yeah! We've seen that look many times before. We can help make everything feel better. One sample if you're interested. Just a pinch."

One of the twins pulled out a small bag with a bit of blue powder, "Pop it in your drink and down the hatch. You'll feel right as rain. The first one is free because we know once you feel that pain-free happiness, you'll come back for more." Reluctantly, Nathan took the small bag and put it in his pocket. The twins nodded at each other and walked away, "Enjoy." A sense of dread flooded his mind as he finished his drink, watching Ivy make her way across the room.

He gave her a smile as she moved closer. He reached under the bar and tried to hide his cane more. "We should really get this cut," she giggled as she ran her fingers through his hair, "Also, stop trying to hide your cane from me. I know you have it, and I encourage you to use it whenever you need additional assistance."

The pair relocated to a table nearby when it became available. Dinner was full of laughter. She made him feel so comfortable that he didn't notice the people around them occasionally staring and talking about them. None of that mattered. He finally found someone who looked past his complexion and accepted him for the man he really was. They spoke of his profession as a hatter and his difficulties as his body grew increasingly tired.

Ivy spoke about the hospital and the new addition they were looking to build. Time felt like it had stopped entirely until Nathan began to look pale. "Are you okay?" she asked quietly, her brow knitting. He nodded slightly, "I'm just tired, that's all. I don't want this to end, though." She blushed and gently bit her lip, "If you would like, we can go back to your place so you can get more comfortable, and I will stay with you for a while." He paid for the meal with a smile, and they set off towards his apartment.

The apartment was on the ground floor, making it easily accessible for him when he needed to use his mobility aids. Inside was a small kitchen and dining room to the left, and straight ahead was ample open space with a dedicated workspace of various styles of hats, fabrics, hat forms, and blocking tools. She wandered over to the work area to take a closer look at his craftsmanship. "Nathan, these are amazing," she gasped, running her fingers along the brim of a black leather top hat adorned with bronze buckles.

Nathan sat on the couch, "Thank you. I enjoy making hats more than anything. Unfortunately, I had to close my shop not long before the transplant. I still have my clients; I just have to work from home now." He sunk into the couch, laying his head back and closing his eyes. His feet began to move. Opening his eyes, he looked down to see Ivy on her knees, removing his shoes, "Darling, you don't have to do that."

"I know, but I want you to be comfortable. I don't mind at all," she beamed, collecting his shoes and placing them next to hers at the front door. Reaching over, she double-checked the lock on the door before returning to the couch. He was half asleep when she gently stroked his cheek, "Let's get you to bed." Lazily, he opened his eyes, and she started to help him to his feet and into the bedroom.

He sat on the bed as she helped him lift and rest his legs on the bed. Laying back, he repositioned the pillow under his head and moved to his side. Carefully, she covered him with his large black comforter. "Ivy," he whispered, "Please don't leave." She looked at him for a minute before moving to turn off the light. Soft, dim puck lights illuminated the base of the floor, allowing him to safely make his way around the apartment at night if he needed to.

Softly, she climbed into bed next to him and lay on her side with her back facing him. Her cheeks burned, and she was glad it was dark enough that he couldn't see how red she must have been. He gently ran his fingers down the length of her arm, "Thank you for accepting me. I know I'm not an attractive man, but you didn't push me away like everyone else has. It means more to me than I could ever express."

Rolling over, she wrapped her arm around his waist and rested her head against his chest, "Who said you're not attractive? Green is my favorite color." Nathan chuckled as he kissed the top of her head and began running his fingers through her hair until he fell asleep.

Ivy rolled over and placed her hand on Nathan's chest. Looking up, she noticed Nathan lying on his back, staring at the ceiling. "I'm so exhausted," he muttered. She sat up, "Did I keep you awake?"

"No, not at all. That was the best sleep I have had in a while. I have a gnawing pain in my abdomen, and I feel too tired to move."

"Is there anything I can do that may help?"

"Not really, but thank you."

"I do have to head home so I can change for my shift. Unfortunately, I work today. I will come back though after if you would like."

"Please do."

With a solemn smile, Ivy leaned over and kissed his forehead, "Of course. Call me right away if you need me." She slid off of the bed and headed towards the door. He let out a heavy sigh as he heard the door latch behind her. His mind drifted back to the blue powder in his pocket. Could it help? He has never taken any form of drug before unless it was prescribed.

Knowing there was a possibility he could end up having a bad experience, he took comfort in knowing that she would be back in a while. Fighting to get comfortable, he readjusted himself, tucking the pillow she slept on under his arm and leaning against it, trying to take some of the pressure off his back. Laying in the warmth of the sun, he drifted to sleep.

He wasn't asleep for long before the pain in his abdomen woke him back up. Giving into temptation, he rolled over, grabbed the bottle of water from the nightstand, and pulled out the small bag of blue powder. Propping himself up on his elbow, he dumped the powder in his mouth and washed it down with a few large gulps. He placed the empty bag and bottle of water back on the nightstand and laid back down, staring at the ceiling. It didn't take long before his body felt so heavy he couldn't move. He closed his eyes.

The warmth of the sun made him open his eyes. The trees above him gently swayed in the wind as the clouds slowly drifted across the soft sky. He smiled and rubbed his face with his hands. Pulling his hands away, he noticed something very different. Slowly, he sat up and lifted his arms. His pain was gone. Not only did he feel okay, the pigment of his skin wasn't green anymore. He sat there in disbelief. The twins were right.

A younger girl popped over, sat on the grass before Nathan, and smiled at him. The sun bounced off her curls, making them appear gold. "Are you new? You are, aren't you!" she exclaimed, her pale blue eyes sparkling, "Callum! Come look! There's a man here!" A laugh echoed from the woods around them, "Yes darling, I'm sure there is."

She gently touched Nathan's arm, "No, Cal! There really is. I can touch him." Hurried steps filled the air as a man with bright red wild hair rushed out of the woods, "March, move back." Callum came to a stop between March and Nathan, "Why are you here?"

"I was given a blue powder to try. They said it would take away my pain, and it did. Now I'm here…wherever here is."

Callum relaxed and helped March to her feet, "I see. How much did they give you?" He turned and extended a hand towards Nathan, offering to help him up. "Just a pinch. Not much," he explained, accepting the offer of assistance, not entirely sure he would be able to stand on his own. He could. All of the pain and fatigue had left his body. An incredibly large smile crossed Callum's face as he tilted his head towards the woods, "Come back with us. You'll like it here." With a nod, Nathan began following Callum as March skipped next to them.

"What they gave you is known as Wonderland. I'm not sure who gave it to you or why, but it helps people feel normal again, even if only for a little while. Typically, after a few small experiences here, people choose to stay."

"You can choose to stay?"

"You can. It requires a lethal dose, however. Every time, you come right back here. Same people, same places. It's like an alternate reality. Some of us were forced here against our will, but ultimately, it was for the best."

After walking for a bit, the group came to another clearing in the woods where there was a picnic set up. March ran over, sat down, and smiled at the men, "Will you join us? I always pack too much, so we have enough for sure." Callum nodded at Nathan and took a seat next to March. With a smile, Nathan joined them. They ate and had basic conversation, learning about Nathan and his profession as a hatter.

"Cal, can I go pick flowers to take home?" March asked, looking over at the flowers that were blooming at the edge of the clearing near a large glassy lake. "You may just remember, if you need me, cover your eyes and let me know," he responded with a soft smile. March popped up and ran over to the flowers. "Is she your daughter?" Nathan asked, watching her inspect the flowers closely. Callum laughed, "Gods no. I'm older, but not old enough to be her father at all. We were in the same facility, and I couldn't stomach what they were doing to her, so I stepped in. They forced her here, so I followed suit. I couldn't let her be alone again."

Callum bounced his foot, listening to the facility directory lecture him. With a yawn, he ran his hands through his bright red hair. A knock at the door caused the director to stop talking and redirect his attention. The door opened. Sara, one of the psychiatric nurses, stood next to a younger girl with blond curls. He could tell she was scared by how she gripped her tattered pink rabbit to her chest.

He sat up straight and winked at the girl. She couldn't have been more in her mid-teens. "Here is the transfer, sir," Sara stated, handing the folder to the director. The girl blushed and looked at the floor. "She's a cutie," the director remarked, looking at the girl over his thick-rimmed glasses. Callum immediately shot him a glare. The director looked at him and pointed at the door, signifying for him to leave. Callum stomped to his feet, "She's a friggin child!" Sara quickly grabbed Callum's arm and pulled him towards the door. "She's fine. I won't leave her, Cal," she whispered, pushing him out of the office.

Once the paperwork was completed, Sara began giving the girl a tour of the facility. At the end of the tour, they entered the recreational room. Sitting up in a high window was the same man from before. The setting sun shining through his hair made it look like his head was engulfed in flames. "That fireball in the window is Callum," Sara joked as the girls stopped near the window. Callum looked down at the girls, and smiling, he hopped out of the window. "Callum, this is March."

He tilted his head to the side, "March? Like the month?" Sara nodded in response. He looked at the girl and realized she wasn't even looking at him. Her gaze was fixated on something past him. There was nothing there. He slowly knelt before her and stroked her cheek with his thumb. "Hey, darling, are you alright?" he said in a low voice. Without turning her head, she slowly looked towards him, "S-sorry."

With a wide grin, he gently tucked a few loose curls behind her ear, "No need to apologize, kiddo. If you ever need anything, let me know. It doesn't matter if it's in the middle of the night. I'm here, okay." Shyly, she nodded and turned her focus to the ground. Her name was called at the medication window, causing her to glance up at Sara. "Go ahead. They will explain the medication to you and what you need to keep an eye out for, as well as confirm your identity. We will wait for you here," Sara smiled as she waved in the direction of the window. Slowly, she made her way towards the window.

"Sara, why is she here?"

"Hallucinations and suicide attempts."

"Shit. She's just a kid."

"Yeah. Her parents got tired of having to keep an eye on her, so they called the facility to see if we had room for her."

Callum flopped on the couch and looked at the ceiling, "I can keep an eye on her. Someone has to. She's not safe here with the male staff." Sara sighed, sitting next to him, "Unfortunately, you're right. I can't be here all the time either, but when I am here, I will also keep an eye on her." March made her way back to the couch and smiled at Callum. "Listen, if the meds they give you ever start making you feel bad in any way, tell Sara or me immediately. It's not uncommon to get the wrong medication." He said in a low voice, with Sara nodding in agreement.

Sara excused herself, explaining she had patients that needed to be checked on, leaving March with Callum. He motioned for her to sit with him on the couch. As she sat down, he noticed the scars on her arms, and his heart sank. Reaching over, he gently ran his fingers across a few scars and whispered, "You must be careful about who you trust here. The male attendants are not your friends, and I would advise you to do what you can to not be alone with them. A lot of the patients love gossip, so if you tell them anything personal, prepare for everyone to know. We lock our doors at night. Staff can get into any room, but this keeps patients out. I never lock my door, so as I said, if you need me at any time, you have access to me."

Not saying a word, March nodded. The bell rang for dinner. Callum guided his new companion through the process of dinner time, explaining everything as they went. They sat together at a table and ate the slop of the night that was provided for them.

"Um, why are you here, if you don't mind me asking? You seem okay."

"I'm a kleptomaniac. I'm also known as a cat burglar because of it."

"Cat burglar?"

"A lot of people seem to think that if they put their valuables on the second floor or higher, the windows don't need to be locked. I'm proof that that isn't true. People like me are considered cat burglars because we steal from higher areas. They got tired of arresting me, so I ended up here and not in prison because of my mental disorder."

March suddenly jerked, looking at her food and dropping her spoon. Noticing the look of terror on her face, Callum began to rub her back gently. He leaned in close and whispered, "Cover your eyes if you need to. You're okay, I'm here." Squeezing her eyes shut, she took a few deep breaths, trying to calm down. He kept rubbing her back until she began eating again. It was apparent tonight was going to be rough for the girl. Such a strange new location with very specific rules was guaranteed to make adjusting difficult.

When dinner finished, he walked her through the clean-up, then back to her room. He sat on her bed, keeping her company as she began unpacking the few things she brought. "They are going to call lights out soon. If you leave your room and turn left, the last door on the right is mine if you need me. I personally will never turn you away. The staff may stop you if they catch you in the halls after lights out, so you'll have to be quick. I will leave you now. Try to get some rest, darling, and I will be back first thing in the morning."

March watched Callum open his door and give her one final wave before disappearing inside. "Lights out; remember to lock your door," a staff member stated, walking down the hall. She locked the door and sighed. Climbing into her bed, she pulled the thin blanket up to her chin and placed the pillow over her head. She preferred to sleep this way because the materials added a small amount of weight on top of her, making her feel safe. Pulling her pink rabbit up under her chin, she closed her eyes and fell asleep.

To Callum's surprise, March adjusted quickly to the new environment. She followed his advice and kept close to him when she needed to. He protected her, and she provided him peace and stability. March was the only one who could effortlessly calm him down when things were getting out of hand.

March sat under a tree in the gated yard while Callum gently brushed her hair. The gentle breeze offset the heat from the sun perfectly. Noticing Sara walking quickly towards them, March waved, "Sara! Are you going to join us? It's really nice out here today." She sat down next to the pair, "I can't stay. I just really needed to talk with you two, especially you, Cal." He shot her a puzzled look.

Sighing, she spoke in a low voice, "They are implementing a new drug as a method of control. I don't know much about it, but I have seen how quickly patients can overdose on it. If you get out of line, that's their new first line of sedation. All I know is that it comes in as a blue powder, and they mix it with a carrier to inject it.

All of the attending staff carry at least one syringe of it. Please be careful. I have a gut feeling things are going to take a bad turn, and I don't want to see anything happen to either of you." With a nod, she quickly stood up and made her way back to the building.

"We've been good though, right, Cal? We shouldn't have anything to worry about," the girl stated proudly. At that moment, he was glad she was facing away from him, "Yes, darling. We should be fine." Fear had engulfed every fiber of his being, and his heart burned. He knew now, more than ever, they were in danger.

Every time she had an episode, he overheard the guards remarking about how they could get rid of her. Her episodes couldn't be tracked. There was no warning before they happened. He needed to stay closer to her than he had been. The attendants with a new drug were as chaotic as a puppy with a new toy. They would find any reason to use it, mainly to see what it would do but mostly to see how much someone could take.

After dinner, March curled up on the bean bag chair in the corner of the recreational room and read a book as usual. Callum sat watching the news, keeping her in his view. Even though he wasn't able to be out in the world, he tried to keep up with current events. It allowed the facility to feel less like a prison for him.

Without warning, he caught a glimpse of March flail, accidentally tossing the book that was in her hand. He quickly shifted his gaze to her as she covered her face with her hands and began to whimper. Scrambling to his feet, he darted over to her and pulled her from the bean bag chair and into his arms. Sitting on the floor, holding her in his lap, she wiggled and buried her face into his shirt.

Carefully, he began stroking her hair and rocking back and forth. It didn't take long before she was crying hysterically. He knew better than to try and ask her questions, she wasn't able to communicate. She would let him know what happened when she was ready and able. Right now, the most important thing was ensuring her she was safe.

Overhearing what happened, Sara swiftly made her way to Callum and knelt beside him. "What can I do to help?" she whispered. He shook his head, "We just have to wait. Can you help me get her to her room? It's quieter there, and she might feel safer." She helped him to his feet so he didn't have to release the crying girl and walked them to her room.

Once inside, they made sure March was wrapped tightly in her blanket and laid her on her bed. It was almost time for lights out. Sara went to get March's medication as Callum gently climbed into bed behind her. Wrapping his arm around the girl, he nestled his face in her curls. The faint, comforting smell of rose and nag champa filled his nose.

After a while, the crying stopped, and her breathing returned to normal. There was a knock on the door before it opened. "It's time for lights out. You need to return to your room, Callum," the attendant stated flatly. He kissed the back of her head, "Come to my room when they leave. I don't want you to be alone tonight." He lifted himself over her and wiped the remnants of tears from her face as he winked. She watched as he left and locked the door behind him.

March wiggled out of her blanket when the hallway fell silent, and she walked to the door. She opened it as quietly as she could and looked around. No one was there. She took a deep breath and began walking as quietly as she could towards Cal's room. "Sneaking around after hours? Naughty, naughty." She froze. Against her better judgment, she looked behind her to see a male attendant closing the gap between them at a rapid pace.

Grabbing her by the throat, he used his foot to swipe her feet out from below her and pin her to the ground. She was cut off mid-scream. The attendant climbed on top of her, using his free arm to rip her shirt. She desperately tried to scream or at least make some noise.

Hearing the strange sound that came from the hall, Callum sprang out of bed. He was waiting for her, and the sound made him incredibly uneasy. Opening the door, he saw the attendant pinning March to the floor, ripping at her clothes. Not wasting any time thinking, he dashed down the hallway and kicked the attendant in the jaw, not anticipating the attendant would trigger his alarm.

He gently sat the girl up and removed his shirt, "Put this on, sweetheart. I've got you." Dozens of staff members flooded the hallway, and immediately, the blame was placed on Callum. Two security guards grabbed him by the arms and pulled him away from March. A nurse walked over and knelt down by the terrified girl and lifted her chin, "Well, this won't do. Miss, we're going to help you calm down."

The nurse pulled a syringe filled with an odd blue mixture from her scrub pocket and, using her thumb, popped off the cap. Callum began to scream and break his arms free from the guards as the nurse firmly grasped the girl's chin. Without hesitation, she slipped the needle into the interior jugular vein and depressed the plunger.

March looked at Callum, tears cascading down her cheeks moments before the concoction took over. Her eyes rolled back in her skull as her body fell to the floor and began convulsing. Pale blue foam erupted from her mouth, and the nurse stood up and took a few steps back.

Callum furiously headbutted one of the guards and managed to pull away from the other. Rushing to the girl, he slid on his knees and tried to steady her head. "No, no, come on sweetheart. I'm here. I'm always here," he whimpered quietly, brushing her curls from her face. Her body reduced to twitching as her eyes fluttered shut. Horrified, he placed his forehead against hers as his tears peppered her face. "I'm coming, sweetheart. I promised I would always be with you," he whispered, kissing her forehead.

Standing, he turned to look at the remaining staff members in the hallway. Staggering towards them, he formulated a plan. Rushing at the one attendant, he grabbed the pen from their scrub pocket and began wildly stabbing them in the neck. In a defensive act, the last remaining attendant pulled their syringe from their pocket and jammed it into Callum's neck.

As the syringe fell to the ground, he backed away and smiled at the attendants. Swaying towards where March lay, he fell to his knees and crawled towards her. Lying next to her, he smiled and ran his thumb across her cheek one last time before closing his eyes.

"They killed you both?" Nathan squeaked, trying to remain quiet. Callum nodded, "It's for the best, honestly. Very rarely does she have to deal with the hallucinations here, and all I have to do is follow her and watch her be the happiest version of herself she can be. I have wanted nothing more than that since we met."

Skipping, March returned to the men holding two handfuls of flowers. As she sat down, she held them out to both men. "Thank you, March, but I can't bring them back with me. Will you keep them until I return?" Nathan asked with a smile. She tilted her head and blinked, "you're leaving?" He looked over at Callum. He hadn't thought about it before, but what if he didn't leave?

"How much did you take?" Callum asked, placing the flowers in the basket. "It wasn't much. Just a pinch." "You'll leave soon then. That's not enough to keep you here. If you decide to return, you'll end up with us again. No one knows how it works; it just does." Nathan had to go back. Ivy wasn't with him, and he needed to talk to her about what was happening. Deep down, he knew she would be furious when she found out, but he needed this. He needed to feel whole again.

Callum started packing up the picnic, "March, why don't we show him the town? I don't know how much time he has left, but I think he'd like it." Her eyes lit up at the suggestion. She grabbed Nathan's hand and began leading him towards the town. Callum chuckled, "Easy, kiddo. If we don't get to show him everything this time, I feel like we'll see him again."

The town center was relatively small. A handful of cobblestone shops had been built in a large circle. The fountain at the center served as a meeting spot for a majority of the town's children. Black iron streetlamps stood near their corresponding benches. In the distance stood a large, elaborate castle brilliantly colored red and gold.

"There's a castle?" Nathan questioned. "Oh yes!" March beamed, "The King and Queen are absolutely wonderful! Maybe we could take you to meet them one time." The trio sat on a bench by the fountain. This place reminded Nathan of something you would read about in a children's book. The townsfolk greeted each other with smiles and waves. Everyone seemed so pleasant.

Feeling feverish, Nathan rested his head in his hands. "Are you alright?" March asked, looking concerned. Callum took her hand and squeezed it lightly, "He's alright, darling. His visit is just coming to an end." She carefully moved in front of Nathan and knelt before him, "Does it hurt?" Slowly looking up at her, he flashed a soft smile, "No, things just look a bit blurry." Tears streamed down her face as she watched him disappear.

Nathan awoke to Ivy softly running her fingers through his hair. Despite being greeted by her warm, soft smile, his heart sank. "Are you okay? Your heart rate was really low, and I couldn't wake you," she whispered as a tear streamed down the side of his face.

"I'm alright, but I need to have a conversation with you. You have to listen to me fully before responding in any way," he stated flatly, forcing a slight smile. He sat up in his bed with her assistance and explained what he took and why. Her eyes widened, and her mouth fell open slightly. It took every ounce of her being not to yell at him.

"Absolutely not. Nathan, what if it messed with your medication or made your condition worse?"

"I didn't expect you to understand."

"You're right. I could never understand exactly, but all I can do is offer my assistance in the ways I know to try and help you."

"I will try anything to stop the pain, Ivy. This did. I could move freely and was treated like a normal person."

"It wasn't real."

Nathan felt his heart twinge at the reminder that it wasn't real. He wanted more than anything for it to be real, but he also wanted her to be a part of it with him. He didn't want to be alone there. She sighed and walked out of the room. The reaction she had to him using the drug was to be expected. She didn't live in constant pain. His daily struggle was his and his alone; no one could fathom his agony. He also didn't want to disappoint the only woman who loved him.

Still, his mind drifted to the twins. He needed to find them again. The rest of the night was quiet. Neither person said much to the other as they did their routine. "I need to go home, but I don't know if I can leave you here by yourself now," Ivy finally said, looking up from the nursing resource text she was reading, "I have to get my scrubs washed and ready for my shift tomorrow, but I need to know you won't do this again."

He shook his head, "That small bag was all I had." She sighed and rubbed her face, "Okay. That powder brought your heart rate low enough, I almost couldn't tell you were still alive. It was terrifying. If you did it again, you might not be as lucky", she gathered her things and placed them in her bag. With a soft kiss, she made her way out the door.

He sat in silence. The knowledge of Wonderland's existence gnawed at his brain like a mouse desperately trying to escape a cage. Unable to stand it any longer, using his cane for stability, he grabbed his coat and walked out the door. Hoping he would see the twins at the bar, he went to the restaurant. Sitting at the bar, he ordered a glass of water and waited.

"Ready for another round?" a voice chirped behind him. Closing his eyes, Nathan slowly nodded. "Oh, ho! How much this time? A sample size?" a twin stated, leaning against the bar and looking at the distraught man. "No, that's not enough anymore, is it? Not anymore," the other twin moved closer to Nathan's opposite side. "Permanent," he said into his glass before letting the chilled liquid dance into his mouth.

The first twin's mouth dropped open as the second raised an eyebrow at the unexpected response, "That escalated quickly. Why permanent?"

"Because there is less for me here than there is there."

"A bold decision."

"A coward's decision. Why waste time here in pain knowing that I'm dying when I can happily create for people who appreciate my talents there?" Nathan remarked, swirling the remaining liquid in his glass, "In time, she will forget me, and hopefully, I will keep myself busy enough that I won't have to deal with the fact I made the choice to leave her."

The twins nodded and handed the man a larger bag, "The best way to do this is to add half to a tall glass of water and chug it. After that, I would suggest a few sleeping pills. Wait a few minutes, then repeat with the second half. This won't be pleasant at all, but the sleeping pills will help it pass. After the second glass, go to bed." With a pat on the back, the twins walked away. In possession of what he came for, Nathan tucked the contents into his jacket pocket and made his way back home.

Closing the door, he stalled before turning the lock. There was no reason to lock his door anymore. Tears laced his eyes as he made his way to the counter. The counter always had a notebook and pen ready for any new hat ideas he had throughout the day. The pages were filled with crude sketches and notes of various fabrics and colors, except this one. This page would forever contain the explanation of why he chose to leave, assuring Ivy there was nothing she could have done differently.

A gnawing pain took over his lower abdomen like a raging storm, causing him to double over. He wrapped his arms around himself and laid his head on the countertop, waiting for it to subside. "No more," he whispered as tears puddled in the corner of his eye before sliding down his nose. When he was able to move again, he took a few labored breaths as he used his cane to hoist himself from the chair.

As quickly as he could, he started gathering the items suggested by the twins and laying them out on the counter. A smile formed as he watched the blue powder swirl and dance in the glass of water, ultimately turning it into the color of the ocean. Once the powder dissolved, he took the glass, gave it one final swirl, and tossed the contents to the back of his throat.

Unsure of the amount of time he had left, he quickly took the sleeping pills and refilled the glass. He dumped the powder in the glass and didn't bother to watch it. This time, he slowly hobbled to the bedroom with the glass and notebook in his hand. Placing the notebook on the nightstand, he downed the second glass and set it down.

It didn't take long before his head felt heavy and his vision blurred. Laying back on the bed, he watched as the fan above him swayed back and forth. His lungs felt full, causing him to begin coughing and gasping. Slowly, the coughing stopped. The fan stopped rocking, and Nathan closed his eyes.

Guilt plagued Ivy as she worked the next day. She knew she should have approached the situation better, but she was caught off guard by the lengths he was willing to go to in search of relief. She thought about calling him on her break but decided against it. Clocking out from her shift, she gathered her things and made her way to Nathan's apartment.

A lump formed in her throat as the distance between her and his door diminished. Swallowing hard, she inserted her key into the door of the apartment. It was unlocked. Dread pricked every fiber of her being as she slowly opened the door. The kitchen light was on, but it was empty. The deafening silence hung heavily in the still apartment.

Looking towards the bedroom, she froze. The bedroom light was off, but she could make out the curves of his body lying in the bed in the moonlight. Dropping her bag to the ground, she whispered, "Nathan, darling?" Nothing. Slowly, she walked into the room and climbed onto the bed. Crawling over to him, she saw how peaceful he was in the pale moonlight. Running her fingers through his hair, she could feel the chill of his skin. It told her all she needed to know.

Tears streamed down her face as she made the call that her heart begged not to have to make. Hanging up, she lay next to him and began to cry hysterically. She sat by numbly as she watched the paramedics go through their procedures and began to remove Nathan from the bed. One of them picked up the notebook and read it.

With a solemn look, he turned it over and handed it to Ivy, "Not now, but when you're ready." Covering Nathan, the men removed him from the apartment, leaving Ivy to sit silently on the bed. Holding his shirt to her chest, she turned the notebook over.

My dearest rabbit,

I am so sorry. Now that I know there is a way I can be free of pain and live happily, I cannot stay here anymore. You have done so much for me, and I loved the time I was able to be with you. The blue powder, Wonderland, is my only key to true happiness and relief. There are no words I can say to make you understand; I would have to show you. In the restaurant where we had dinner, near the bar, there is a set of twins. They can help you if you want to join me, in Wonderland.

You will forever have my heart.

Wrapping herself in his shirt, she cried herself to sleep, holding his pillow.

The sun burned Ivy's eyes the following day. Still numb from the night before, she knew what she had to do. She buttoned up his shirt and tied the bottom, so it fit better. She threw her hair into a messy bun, slipped her feet into her shoes, grabbed her bag, and left the apartment. Not knowing exactly how to find them, she made her way to the restaurant and sat at the bar.

After nearly an hour, she had almost given up when she noticed two men across the bar smiling at her. Was it them? They looked at each other and nodded. Quickly, they stood up and made their way over to her. "If this isn't the look of pure heartbreak, I don't know what is," One said, leaning on the bar on her right side. "I need what you gave him," Ivy replied in a voice barely more than a whisper. The second twin raised an eyebrow, "You're not even going to try; just dive right in, huh? In that case, I'll tell you what I told him. Add half to a tall glass of water and chug it. After that, I would suggest a few sleeping pills. Wait a few minutes then repeat with the second half. This won't be pleasant at all, but the sleeping pills will help it pass. After the second glass, go to bed."

The first twin produced a bag of blue powder and handed it to Ivy. "You'll find him. You may have to ask around, but he's there," the second stated, tucking a few loose strands of Ivy's hair behind her ear, "He was hoping you would follow him down this path. He's happy now." The twins nodded at each other and made their way out the door.

She buried her face in her hands and took a deep breath. Shoving the bag of powder in her pocket, she tipped the bartender and left. Knowing exactly how she wanted to do this, she wasted no time when she reached the apartment. Immediately, she filled a glass of water and dumped in the powder. Grabbing a spoon, she swished it until the powder dissolved and downed the contents as if she were in a race.

She scrunched her nose at the gritty texture and shook her head, trying not to gag. Shaking it off, she popped two sleeping pills into her mouth and swallowed them dry while filling the next glass of water. Stirring in the powder a little longer did nothing to assist with the gritty feeling left in her mouth after downing the second glass.

She rinsed the glass and left it in the sink. Grabbing the notebook, she made her way to the bedroom. Climbing in bed, she hugged the notebook as she began to feel the effects of the drug. The room started to swirl and sway, causing her to feel as if she was being bounced on the ocean. Ivy squeezed her eyes shut, hoping it would help, but it didn't.

Moments later, she began to cough so violently that she vomited on the floor next to the bed. Gasping for air, she laid back on the pillow and watched as the color began to fade. Still clutching the notebook, she smiled as the numbness set in. Then it was black.

10

Warmth washed over Ivy as if she were coddled in the world's softest blanket. Sighing, she shuffled a bit, stretching her hands wide. Realizing she was running her fingers through the grass, her eyes fluttered open. The sun was high above her, providing warmth. "Well now, what have we here?" a voice purred.

Tilting her head back, she noticed a man with bright red hair looking at her from a tree branch. She sat up, "Where am I?" The man laughed in response and hopped down, "You are here. It's known as Wonderland, but I have a feeling you knew that already." Looking around, she was amazed at the scenery. Brilliantly colored flowers bloomed in droves. The gentle breeze rocked the trees, sending the welcoming scent of oranges through the air.

"I'm looking for someone," Ivy said, looking back at the man, "He's um…green." Tilting his head to the side, he narrowed his eyes at her, "You expect me to believe there are green people?"

"I was told I would be able to find him if I asked around. There's no reason to be rude."

"I'm not the one asking about green men."

"Perhaps he isn't green here. How about a hatter? Do you know any hatters?"

"Ah, now that I do know. In fact, my little March is over with him at the town center as we speak."

"Town center? Will you take me there?"

A frighteningly large grin crossed the man's face as he bowed, "My pleasure. I'm headed there myself." She stood up and followed next to the strange man in silence. A town began to emerge ahead of them, covered in banners and balloons. The smell of freshly baked goods filled the air, accompanied by music and laughter.

"A celebration?" Ivy asked. "Absolutely, the King and Queen will be visiting. They are the most amazing people you could ever meet," The man swooned. Stopping, he pointed at the large fountain with children running around and playing, "Is that your hatter?" A girl with bouncy blonde curls was lying on the edge of the fountain with her head in a man's lap as he hand-repaired the hat he was holding.

Her mouth fell open slightly, utterly stunned at what she saw. Taking her reaction as a yes, the man walked over and knelt beside the girl. "Come, March, he has a visitor," he whispered, lifting the girl. Lazily, she wrapped her arms around the man's neck and pulled herself close to him. Nathan smiled at the sight. Shifting his gaze, he noticed Ivy standing in the crowd.

Setting the hat next to him on the fountain, he stood up and rushed over to her, "Ivy!" Before she could react, he wrapped his arms around her and kissed her forehead. Smiling, he looked down at her and brushed his thumb across her cheekbone. "I really found you," she whispered, still in awe of the man standing before her, "You're so different." He laughed, "I told you darling. This is what I've craved for so long. No pain, no cane, I can move freely, and I'm not discolored. I knew explaining it wouldn't do it justice, you had to see it for yourself, but honestly, I never thought you would."

March opened her eyes and waved with a large smile, "Oh! You must be his rabbit! I'm so glad you joined us. It's a great day too! The King and Queen will be arriving soon; you must meet them!" Callum smiled and set the excited girl down, who wasted no time running over to the couple. Moments later, fanfare joyfully echoed through the town center, announcing the arrival of the King and Queen.

Proudly, they made their way onto the tall stage just past the fountain. They smiled and waved at the crowd as the sun glistened off of the glorious display of gold, white, and red on their attire. March beamed with childlike wonder as she watched the royal family on the stage. Smiling at her, Callum draped his arm across her shoulders and pulled her closer.

They made their opening statements and thanked the citizens for joining in the celebration. Noticing the new faces in the crowd, they welcomed the new inhabitants. Standing behind them was the Queen's younger sister. Her face was as cold as stone as she glared at the crowd. Periodically, she would roll her eyes and cross her arms in disappointment. It was no secret that the sister was jealous of the Queen. She didn't try to hide it. During childish fits, she would often claim to take the throne one day.

As the opening ceremony concluded, the younger sister marched forward, "I have something to add." Everyone froze and looked at her. Their smiles faded. Callum reached over and grabbed Nathan's wrist, pulling him closer. "Something's not right. I don't like this," he whispered. Nathan shifted his gaze from Callum and March to Ivy. The hair on the back of his neck stood on edge as the younger sister walked over to face the Queen.

"I'm tired of living in your shadow. It ends today," she smirked, thrusting her hand into the chest of the Queen. The sound of the Queen's rib cage cracking echoed as the civilians watched in horror. Blood spurted across the sister's face as she pulled her siblings' heart from the gaping wound. The Queen stumbled backward with a look of terror on her face. The King lunged forward, grabbing her before her limp body crashed to the stage floor.

The sister licked at the blood dripping from the pericardium that clung to the heart. Pressing her lips to it, she began to whisper before sinking her teeth into the pulsating organ in her hand. Suddenly, the guards simultaneously dropped to the floor. The sun faded, causing the sky to take on a dreary grey hue. "I am your Queen now," she roared, running a blood-coated hand through her long blonde curls. The destroyed King glanced up at the new, self-proclaimed Queen with tears streaming down his face.

Nathan fell to his knees, coughing violently. "Hey, are you okay? What's happening?" Ivy squeaked, kneeling next to him. He looked up at her, revealing his malnourished, green-tinted appearance. Her heart sank as she ran her fingers through his hair. March began to panic, viciously attempting to climb up Callum. "Close your eyes," he ordered, lifting the girl into his arms.

The guards began stumbling to their feet and looked at the crowd with twitching movements. A few snarled as they looked between the citizens. The new Queen dropped the remainder of the heart to the stage floor. "I have much to discuss with my King," she locked eyes with Ivy and glared, "The citizens are yours. Feed." Swaying her hips, she walked over and grabbed the King by the collar, jerking him to his feet and pulling him off stage.

After a few more twitches, one of the guards lunged forward. He sank his teeth into the neck of a man near the stage, pinning him to the ground. Blood sprayed his face as he began ripping at the skin with little effort. Pulling back his head, tendons snapped, releasing a wad of flesh-speckled muscle. Taking this as a signal to proceed, the remaining guards snarled as they rushed the crowd.

Screams rang out as the civilians struggled to run away. The decorations that filled the town center were ripped apart and speckled red as the sound of screams and snapping bones from the weaker civilians being trampled filled the air. Callum thrusted March at Ivy. "Take her," he ordered as he snatched Nathan to his feet, "Follow me."

Pulling Nathan's arm around his neck, Callum began running towards an alley on the side of town. Ivy stayed close behind Callum. At the end of the alley was a boarded, decaying building. Releasing his friend, Callum pried a few boards from the bottom of the door, "Quick, inside." Ivy pushed March inside the opening without a question and crawled in behind her. After getting Nathan inside, Callum pulled the boards closer and wedged them between the frame and broken pieces of the door.

"I'm not sure how long it will hold, but it buys us a bit of time. Let everyone else leave and let it get darker. I will scout the area from the trees and figure out our next move then." He whispered, making his way to his companions. March began to cry. Callum's heart sank, and he pulled the crying girl closer, "It'll be okay, March." She shook her head, "It won't. I-I can't remember your name. I don't know why I'm here!" He froze. The group looked at each other in shock. With the carnage that took place, none of them realized the new Queen not only took away everyone's happiness but also portions of their memories.

"I don't remember my name either," Callum whispered, "All I know is I was sent to the asylum because of being a kleptomaniac cat burglar that they got tired of arresting." She looked up and wiped the tears from her eyes, "Can I call you Cat? I don't want to call you a burglar." He smiled and kissed her forehead, "Of course." Ivy and Nathan looked at each other. "All I remember is the constant medical procedures, the fact that I love you. You were swift as a rabbit and tried your best to save me, and I was a hatter by trade." Nathan muttered. March smiled, "Okay, so Hatter for you, and we can call her Rabbit."

Ivy nodded, "If that's what you'd like, I'm fine with it." The girl stopped crying now that she could identify everyone. Callum ushered everyone further into the decaying building as the thundering sound of people running became louder. He stood up and began to quietly look around the building, checking to see if there was anything they could use to their advantage. Opening a door, he noticed it led down to a basement.

Spotting an oil lamp hanging next to the door, he carefully lit it and descended into the darkness. Downstairs contained a few rooms with beds. With a new plan in mind, he returned to the group. "Hey, Rabbit, can you help me move a few mattresses downstairs?" he called from the doorway. She followed him downstairs, and they began to move the mattresses to the open area in front of the rooms.

"We can sleep down here. We'll be more hidden, and it will help keep everyone safe while I scout later." Callum patted Ivy's shoulder, "Let's get everyone down here. We'll have to keep a close eye on March. Based on what happened to Hatter and the fact we lost portions of our memories, I feel like her struggles aren't too far behind." They returned to the remainder of the group and helped them downstairs.

The group lay together on the mattresses in the middle of the floor. Callum fell asleep nearly instantly, with March lying next to him. She lay there looking at Ivy, "I'm scared, Rabbit." Ivy lovingly played with the girl's curls, offering her a gentle smile, "I know, we all are. It'll be okay, though." Nathan buried his face in Ivy's hair and wrapped his arm around her waist, "I didn't want this." She didn't respond.

They lay there in silence, listening to the thunderous rumble of footsteps and screams coming from outside. Eventually, they all fell asleep. No one slept well. The evening was full of tossing and turning. Sometimes, they were awoken by screams; sometimes, it was the sound of buildings surrounding them being destroyed.

March shuddered in her sleep, and her eyes popped open. "Momma?" she whimpered, sitting up. Someone was calling her name. Paying no attention to her sleeping companions, March made her way off the mattresses and up the stairs. "Momma?" She called again, opening the door, "Where are you?" Quietly, she closed the door behind her and walked into the room.

A deep, guttural growl came from behind her. Her eyes widened as she turned around to see a guard standing there, saliva dangling from his blood-stained mouth. Before she could scream, the guard lurched forward, clamping down hard on her trachea. Silent tears cascaded down her face as blood began to seep out of the punctures and down her dress. The guard shook his head before staggering out of the building, dragging the dangling girl with him.

Callum reached over in his sleep. Realizing the girl was gone, he sprung up, "No!" Ivy and Nathan were startled awake. "Cat," Ivy squeaked, "Where is March?" Callum stumbled to his feet and darted up the stairs with the couple not far behind him. Tossing open the door, he stopped dead upon seeing the splotches of blood on the floor. Overcome by an immense pain in his chest, he almost collapsed.

Nathan grabbed his arm and pulled him back up. "Up. We have to move. We can't stay here." Noticing the guards in the room staggering towards them, the group darted to the newly unbarricaded doorway. The ground was now littered with bits of flesh, blood, and bone. Running as fast as they could, they made their way into the woods. The trio didn't stop running until they were on the outskirts of the next town.

"Wha-what do we do now?" Ivy asked, placing her hands on her knees, fighting to catch her breath. Callum hastily brushed the tears from his eyes without turning to his companions behind him, "The only thing we can do now is survive. "

Part 1

Alice stared in the mirror, viciously wiping tears streaming from her eyes. The flickering light in the club's bathroom was starting to piss her off. *This club sucks, but it's better than being home alone.* With a heavy sigh, she tucked her brown hair behind her ears, smoothed her dark blue dress over her curvy hips, and walked out of the bathroom.

The club's people seemed lost in more than just the music. The walls were lined with people staring off into oblivion, utterly unfazed by what was happening around them. Alice sucked in a sharp breath as she watched a man bite into his beer bottle, completely void of emotion. She shook her head and kept walking towards the bar. It was becoming more and more evident that something was terribly wrong. *At least I'm not at home.*

In this poor town, drugs were all the rage. On the nights when the rain never seemed to stop, the citizens would be forced to look for other means of obtaining happiness. In one way or another, they would all try to leave. Whether they were able to do so was always a mystery.

Most of the civilians who attempted to leave the town ended up dying suddenly. It became so continuous that people stopped trying to escape. They also stopped having children, knowing they would be stuck here, rotting away on the inside. Relationships fell apart, and people rarely talked to each other anymore unless it was necessary.

Alice's parents had become so self-involved that they barely remembered she existed, even when she was standing directly in front of them. Many nights, they were found passed out, draped over various pieces of furniture from whatever drug they happened to take that night. One night, cooking was too much of a chore, and her mother didn't even concern herself with checking labels as she threw whatever she grabbed into a pot. The arsenic under the sink found its way into their dinner that night and not to the rats. Unfortunately for Alice, it wasn't enough to kill the three of them.

"That ass!" Alice heard, followed by a howl behind her. Irritated, Alice turned around and placed her hands on her hips. Standing there were two twin brothers with spiked dirty blond hair, looking like they had just stepped off the beach. "Wearing sunglasses in a dark club is a bit obnoxious, isn't it?" Alice snapped, raising an eyebrow. "Not when you have the goods, bae." One brother said, bobbing to the rhythm of the playing music. "Not in the least." added the other. "I'm Dee, and this is my bro Dum." The one who seemed slightly more mature stated, "You seem rather troubled, bae. Want to talk about it?".

"As much as I appreciate it, no," Alice stated flatly as she turned to walk away. Dum reached out and grabbed her hand. "In that case, can we interest you in a journey? Everyone is dying to leave here." "Literally," Dee added, reaching into his pockets. He pulled out a small bag containing light blue powder, "Just a pinch, and you can easily leave this hellhole behind for a while. No more than a pinch. This is called Wonderland. The first one is free because we know you'll be back for more bae. Bliss, pure bliss. Each user experiences something different. It could be a day at the beach, hanging with dead homies, or a club completely fabricated by your mind. It's worth the journey."

Escape from reality has been the only thing Alice has craved for over a decade, just like everyone else. Wonderland must be what everyone who has mentally checked out in the club has taken. She desperately longed for that escape and agreed to give it a try. The brothers smiled at each other and ordered Alice a shot.

Dee grabbed a pinch of powder and dropped it in her shot. She swirled the shot before tossing it to the back of her throat. The boys sat her down in a chair and explained that it was best to stay seated for safety reasons.

Waiting for Wonderland to take effect, Alice spun the empty shot glass in circles. The sounds of laughter started filling the void around Alice, but she noticed no one was laughing. Her face began to feel flushed as her chest squeezed what seemed like every bit of oxygen out of her lungs. With a few rather violent coughs, Alice began to lose consciousness. She laid her head on the bar to steady the swaying and watched as all the colors faded. *Still better than home...*

A warm feeling washed over Alice as she started to regain consciousness. She could hear the wind gently blowing through the trees in such a way that they sounded almost as if they were singing. Slowly, she opened her eyes and was immediately stunned by the brightly colored lush trees and flowers around her. The sun's warmth was something she hadn't felt in what seemed like a lifetime. A small smile formed on her face but quickly faded when she noticed a man lying against a tree a few yards ahead.

He had a large top hat sitting on top of shoulder-length black hair. His shirt was a dingy white with straps and a few holes that matched his pants as if he had gotten them from a local asylum's garage sale. His face was sunken and pale with a sickly green tint. Against her better judgment, Alice stood up and cautiously approached the man. As she moved closer, she noticed he was completely still, eyes open and not blinking. Daring not to get too close for fear of what could happen, she squatted a few feet from him. "Well, you look rather rough."

No response. Not even a flinch at the sound of her voice. Irritated, she walked over and nudged his knee with her boot. Within a split second of contact, she had noticed he was now looking directly at her. "You shouldn't be here," he stated with a deep, raspy voice. "This is all a mistake." Alice rolled her eyes. "Nice to meet you too? Anyway, I'm Alice. What is this place?" Letting his gaze drop back to the ground, the man sighed, "I don't know where there is to you, but this is my hell."

"Rather dramatic, I'd say. What's your name, and why are you just lying here acting like you are dead?" Alice demanded, folding her arms. "You're not from here, are you? Just like them. Of course, they are gone now...a-and my Rabbit-" The man sat up looking at Alice. "Please help me find my Rabbit. It wasn't her fault. If I wasn't so defiant, she would have been safe. They call me Hatter.". "To my understanding, Hatter is a profession and not a name. How did you lose a rabbit?" The more questions Alice seemed to ask, the more confused she ended up becoming. She sat on the grass, looking at the sickly man. It was apparent to her now that she was high from the drug she had taken from the twins.

"Indeed. I have no other name. If I did, I have been called Hatter for so long that it is no longer relevant. I didn't lose Rabbit. She was taken from me." Hatter pulled at the ends of his hair with scarred fingers. The look in his dark eyes hollowed as he began to dissociate again. Convinced she would never get anywhere with Hatter; she stood up and turned to walk away. "You are one of the rudest creatures I have ever had the displeasure of laying eyes on! "A loud voice erupted behind Alice, shaking her to the core. She knew it couldn't have been Hatter, but there was no one else with them, or so she thought.

"Our world isn't yours. No, you don't belong here, but since you are here, you could at least make yourself useful. Hatter dissociates. It's the only way he has learned to deal with losing Rabbit. The proper inhabitants of this world cannot die. Pain and scars remain, no matter how vicious the attempt is, but death never comes. On the other hand, as with other visitors before you, you can die, so I suggest you mind your attitude, little girl."

Standing next to the vacant Hatter was another man. His lean figure donned a professional button-up shirt and slacks. The actual level of importance of this man was yet to be determined. His level of professionalism was offset by his freckles and wild hair that made his head seem as if it was engulfed in flames. His intense emerald eyes pierced right through Alice, chilling her to the bone.

"I'm unsure what to do to help, but I can try. I-I'm just confused about where I am and what is happening. "Alice said dryly. "I took a drug, and this is where I woke up." The tense air was suddenly filled with a large laugh. "Oh, we know exactly what you did, girl. Since you said you'd help, we should get moving." He snapped at Hatter, whose eyes shifted towards him. "Cat..."

"Up Hatter. We are leaving."

The trio moved along in silence. Cat stayed in the trees like a primal Tarzan just ahead of Alice and Hatter. The trees were the best way to determine that there was no immediate danger ahead. Wonderland was intoxicatingly beautiful to anyone who ventured there. The trees sang in the breeze as the flowers seemed to smile at those who passed by them. "Up!" Cat yelled quickly, thrusting his hand down towards Alice and Hatter. Without additional warning, Hatter hoisted Alice up to Cat, who demanded she keep quiet and behind him.

From the trees, Alice could hear the screams. Once you were above the first row of branches, you could see the rot and decay that was Wonderland. Below the trees, three men were walking towards Hatter. Their bodies swayed with their movements as if they were possessed. A mixture of saliva and blood trailed down their faces as they moved closer. One was dragging the remains of yet another visitor behind them by the hair. The victim's expression of pure terror was permanently embedded on their face. Judging by the sections of serrated muscles, it was obvious to see where the men were feeding on the victim. A section of the arm ripped from the body and was carelessly left behind after becoming lodged in a downed branch.

"Hatter." A man gurgled and hissed as they passed him. Hatter's expression was blank as he looked at the men passing by covered in the blood and ripped bits of flesh from their victim that still lingered. Cat carefully turned to Alice and pressed his lips to her ear, "Those are a few of the guards. They are all numbered, and their sole purpose is to find those who do not belong here.

The Queen keeps all her guards always drugged with an appetite enhancer. The enhancer helps to guarantee they will find outsiders and rid our world of them." Alice looked as if her eyes were about to bulge from her head. Her blood ran cold. Cat countered her grave expression with a demonically large smile that nearly stretched from ear to ear, pulling the skin on his face tight nearly to the point of ripping it open.

"It hasn't always been like this. Our current Queen only obtained her position by devouring the heart of the previous Queen." Cat said, lowering Alice back down to Hatter, "To make matters worse, she tortured the King into submission. He stands by her side, but only because he knows what will happen if he denies her." As they ventured deeper into the woods, the beauty of Wonderland started to fade. The birds flying overhead made subtle sounds that sounded like they were sobbing rather than singing.

Suddenly, Hatter came to a stop. He started breathing erratically as his eyes darted around the woods. Cat jumped down from the tree and firmly grabbed Hatter's face with both hands. "Stay with us. She's not here." Tears started to stream down Hatter's cheeks, and he looked at Cat. Even though Hatter was looking at him, Cat could tell he was looking directly through him. "She's crying," Hatter whispered. With a heavy sigh, Cat released Hatter's face, "More than likely she is, but she is not here. Whatever you are seeing, I'm afraid, isn't real... Maybe we should rest a bit before we continue."

Hatter slid down a tree trunk and sat motionless on the ground. Alice took a seat next to Cat on a lower branch. The ground was covered in dead leaves, rotten foliage, and occasional splashes of blood, and Alice would be damned if she was going to sit on any part of it. After watching Hatter dissociate completely, she turned to Cat and quietly asked what caused Hatter to be the way he was. Cat scoffed, "He used to be so happy, and the children loved him." The immediate confusion on Alice's face at the word children urged Cat to explain further while they were resting.

"He's here, He's here!" a boy screamed, running through the streets. All the children began laughing and quickly got up, discarding their previous actions. Hatter laughed as the kids all circled him. "Wait, wait. Let's sit by the fountain. I promise I will have enough balloons this time!" Hatter laughed, leading the children to the fountain in the middle of the courtyard. He spent the next few hours creating elaborate balloon hats and swords for the children to play with. Once the kids were occupied, he set to work repairing the necessary hats and sketching requests for the various townspeople.

A chubby girl with bouncy black curls plopped onto Hatter's lap, "Hatter, have you met the new Queen yet? I heard she's pretty.". "I have not. I am supposed to meet with her and the King before I leave today," Hatter replied, tilting his head. The girl stuck her nose in the air and crossed her arms, "You better not think she's prettier than me, Hatter!" The crowd laughed as Hatter, with a playful look of shock, wrapped his arms around her, "Oh goodness no! Not more than you!"

"What about me?" The voice was playful yet sensual, immediately making Hatter's heart flutter. He glanced over to see a woman smiling at him with long dark red hair that looked deadly against her pale skin. Her eyes looked as if the gods felt that sapphires were perfectly acceptable to see with. He gently moved the girl to the ground and stood up, "Never more than you, my Rabbit." Hatter and Rabbit spent the next few hours talking and catching up before he was due at the castle.

Rabbit sat against a tree, running her fingers through Hatter's hair as he lay his head in her lap, "I don't like that you have to meet with the Queen. I don't trust her." Hatter shifted to look at Rabbit better, "It's part of the profession, darling. What makes you feel so uneasy?" She looked at the sky," She killed her sister and ate her heart. Who does that? It's ferocious! She doomed her own blood to a life of wandering until the roots bind her feet to the ground, claiming her as a part of it! It's not okay! I-"

Hatter jumped up and immediately pulled Rabbit into his arms, "Easy, my love, easy. I agree; it was a terrible thing for her to do. I don't know anything about this Queen, but I promise I will stay alert around her. I must go, but don't forget about our lunch plans tomorrow before I leave." Hatter interrupted Rabbit's smile with a deep kiss that he trailed down her neck. With a final kiss on her forehead, he grabbed his bag and headed towards the castle.

"Keep your wits about you, Hatter. She's not an honorable Queen in any sense of the word." A voice said flatly, following beside Hatter as he neared the castle.

"So, you've met her?"

"Aye. I don't trust her to the point that I will attend this meeting with you so that you aren't alone if things start to take a nasty turn," Cat replied, walking in tandem with Hatter, "She scares Rabbit. The only time they saw each other, The Queen gave her a deadly glare, which set off a ton of red flags. I've been watching her since."

The guards stared at Hatter as he made his way to the throne room. The King sat quietly, gazing at the ground, refusing to look up. Hatter could faintly see the King wearing makeup to hide the bruises that hugged his neckline. The Queen shifted her weight on her throne and crossed her legs. Her curly, long blonde hair seemed to embrace all of her curves in such a way that you couldn't help but be mesmerized by her form. Hatter clenched his jaw and averted his gaze when she leaned forward, folding her arms under her ample breasts, "So, you're the Hatter."

Hatter immediately knew he was in danger and was glad Cat was nearby. "I am. My services were requested," Hatter said dryly. The King glanced at Hatter in a way that begged him to run. The Queen stood and walked towards him, swaying her hips as she did, "They were." After circling Hatter, she stopped before him and licked the side of her mouth, "I do require your services, but not as a mere Hatter. You see, the King is useless to me in more ways than one, and after hearing how everyone loves you, I have decided that you will be more than suitable to take his place."

"I appreciate your consideration; however, I must respectfully decline. Being a Hatter is my life, and I would ask for nothing more than to continue fulfilling my role and being with the people." Hatter responded calmly. He was so terrified he could feel the tangy taste of vomit welling up inside, fighting to be released. The Queen narrowed her eyes at him. The atmosphere around her suddenly fell dead as an evil presence crept over Hatter. "Dismissed." the Queen hissed as she turned around and stomped away, "King, I expect you and the guards in the war room within the hour." Stumbling to his feet while profusely apologizing, the King hurried to gather the guards.

"Go as far as you can and quickly." The King muttered quickly as he rushed past Hatter. Grabbing his bag, he hurried into the courtyard. Cat whistled from the treetops, catching Hatter's attention. Hatter ran into the woods, focusing only in front of him with an occasional glance to ensure he was still following Cat.

Once he could no longer see the castle, Hatter couldn't hold it back as he fell to his knees, and vomit spewed all over the ground before him. Cat sat on a branch, watching his friend below, "I tried to warn you. That Queen is not to be trusted, and I fear we are about to deal with something much more evil than just her overall presence." Assisted by Cat, Hatter returned to his feet and continued toward town.

Hatter's heart was racing. Before he could reach her door, it flew open. He blushed as he noticed how delicately Rabbit's flowy black summer dress gently caressed her curves. Unable to contain her happiness, she raced down the steps and leaped at him. Hand in hand, they made their way to a clearing in the woods behind the town. The trees parted to allow the sun to kiss the flowers below lovingly. They laid the blanket down, and Rabbit sprawled out on top, closing her eyes and taking in the sun. A sigh escaped Hatter as he looked at his Rabbit carefree and happy. Stretching his arms backward in the grass, he closed his eyes, facing the sun.

That pure moment of happiness was quickly shattered as Hatter felt a rope grip around his neck, dragging him backward. Rabbit screamed as leather restraints were clasped around her wrists, breaking the delicate skin underneath. Hatter noticed the men who had restrained them were guards. One of the guards was breathing heavily as he stared at

Hatter in a deranged manner. Saliva was streaming down his chin like a rabid animal. As Rabbit struggled, the leather tightened until a dark red tint took over her hands, and streams of blood ran down her arms as if they had finally found freedom.

Hatter clawed at the rope, ripping open the surrounding skin. The raspy breathing of one of the guards behind him turned into a feral sucking sound as the guard lapped up the trail of saliva seconds before sinking his jagged teeth into Hatter's hand. The guards' action appeared to give the rest permission to begin. Hatter fought in horror as he watched the two guards restraining Rabbit start ripping at her flesh with their nails and releasing her restraints. A guard took the liberty of stilling her screams by impaling the side of her throat with his serrated teeth.

The more she fought, the more they clawed, leaving Hatter haunted by the sloshing sounds of blood spurting from her wounds. The King appeared behind Rabbit and the guards. "Please, my Lord! Please make them stop!" Hatter choked out, struggling against the ropes. Tears streamed down the King's face as he gazed at the blood-stained grass and whispered, "I can't. I'm sorry." Moments after Rabbit fell unconscious, a maniacal laugh filled the clearing like a thick, heavy ooze.

The King brought forth an iron rabbit helmet painted white. "Please forgive me," he whimpered, forcing the helmet onto Rabbit's limp body. The helmet pulled at her hair as sections of skin ripped and folded down her neck, covering her torso in blood. "No one denies me, Hatter." The Queen hissed, walking up beside the King, "If I can't have you bend to my will, you can't have her. Take her away." One of the guards bent his head backward to look at the Queen with blood and bits of mangled flesh dangling from his mouth. The second guard sank his nails into Rabbit's arm above her elbow, breaking off a nail on her bone, and limped away, dragging her still body through the flowers of the clearing.

Hatter's mouth fell open, watching as his beloved Rabbit was ripped from him. He wasn't convinced he was still breathing as tears cascaded down his face. Knowing that there was no way Hatter could fight back at that moment, the rope was removed from his neck. "I will give you the day to reconsider, Hatter," The Queen laughed as the group retreated through the woods.

Cat slid on his knees over to Hatter and quickly grabbed his bleeding hand. "P-please. Rabbit," Hatter whimpered, fighting to breathe. Cat forcefully ripped a portion of his shirt off to wrap Hatter's mangled hand, "Shh. I know, I know. I saw. You know as well as I do if I had tried to interfere, it would have been disastrous for all of us. I'm so sorry, Hatter, but we will get her back. For now, we need to get out of here before the guards do their rounds. We cannot trust they will have anyone's best interest in mind."

A few days later, Hatter returned to town. The children, once full of glee, now kept their distance from him as they watched him set the finished hats on the side of the fountain. His appearance looked ghastly compared to before. Sharp cheekbones were now visible from Hatter refusing to eat anything since she was taken.

An older man approached him, softly saying, "Hatter, my boy. We are all dreadfully sorry. She meant a lot to all of us. I can only imagine the pain you feel. Please let us know if there is anything we can do to help you. Anything at all. You look like you need a good meal, son. Are you hungry?" He closed his eyes as the tears started to fall, shook his head, and left town.

5

A snapping sound alerted Cat that they weren't alone, "We have to move." The group gathered themselves and continued their journey deeper into the woods. The deeper they ventured, the more intense the odor became, causing Alice to retch, "Dude, what the hell? How can one place go from so welcoming and beautiful to this?" Cat gave Alice his overly stretched-out smile and chuckled, "As I'm sure you have noticed from the guards, outsiders don't exactly make it this far. As for us, this is home now. Mind your footing as we progress, dear Alice; there's no telling what may be on the ground." Alice wrinkled her nose, causing Cat to laugh again as they walked.

"Wait," Cat hissed. Everyone stopped and looked at Cat, who now oddly resembled a terrified mouse that had seen its predator. A few minutes passed before Cat knelt, "Let me go ahead. Both of you stay still and quiet. I see something, but I fear what it leads to will not be pleasant, and before either of you deal with anything that can be avoided, I want to look."

Alice rolled her eyes as she leaned against a tree, "Vague much?". The look Cat gave her warned her she needed to watch her mouth.

With a quick leap, Cat was in the trees and gone. Hatter wasn't the best company, but it was better than being left entirely alone. "So...do outsiders end up here often?" Alice finally asked, breaking the deafening silence. "More than you would think," Hatter responded flatly, "You can always tell the difference between the people who come here willingly and those who are forced. Of course, the ones who are forced here are devoured at a much faster pace. The level of fear that they feel causes glucose levels to spike in their bloodstream, providing a sweeter taste. Cat believes that's another reason why the Queen keeps the guards drugged. The sheer look of them is enough to cause fear in outsiders." She released a sigh, wishing she had just kept her mouth shut.

Cat squatted on a branch and narrowed his eyes. He could see someone with an iron rabbit helmet on their knees digging at the ground. It wasn't their Rabbit, which meant there were more victims. The girl filtered through the rotten flesh, bone, and foliage remnants. Cautiously, he lowered himself to the ground as he attempted to get closer. After a few moments, she stood up, pretended to look around, and trotted deeper into the woods. Knowing she couldn't see through the helmet, he wondered if she could sense that she was being watched.

He followed her for what felt like forever, as silently as possible. Occasionally, she would stop and shift her head around before continuing onward. As they ventured deeper into the woods, they were greeted by horrifying sounds of multiple muffled screams. She continued towards a large building as Cat stopped dead in his tracks. He felt as if all the blood was suddenly drained from his body. The gruesome sight ahead of him was even worse than he had feared, but he was right. What he initially saw led to something much worse. Unfortunately, it couldn't be avoided. "Fuck..." he muttered as he turned and rushed back to his companions.

Cat slowed his run as he approached the rest of the group. Alice noticed how pale he was, so she encouraged him to sit. Cat shook his head slowly, "No. There's more than one. There are dozens, and that's just what I saw on the outside..." Alice tilted her head in confusion. She could tell Hatter was contemplating the information they were just given, as if he had already known the whole story. "It's a farm. I saw a girl with a white iron rabbit helmet in the woods, but I knew it wasn't her, so I didn't want to alarm you, Hatter. I followed her, and she led me to a fucking farm. Dozens of girls in iron rabbit helmets. They can't see or speak. Their screams are muffled, which explains where all the missing girls went. Some seem quite young as well. Hatter, March may be there." Cat's words trailed off as if he became lost in thought.

"Wait, who is March?" Alice quietly questioned. "March was a young girl who was forced here. She was badly abused and drugged. She had the cutest little dimples and bouncy curls. She was as sweet as a flower and never deserved the scars she carried. She went missing, and if she's there, she was forced even further into a hellish loop." Hatter had begun digging his nails into his flesh as he scratched at his wrist. Noticing Hatter's excoriation, Cat put his hand around Hatter's wrist, "Let's go."

Trying to ignore the sights and smells around her, Alice couldn't help but taste the pungent tang of vomit that was threatening to make its appearance. As they got closer to the farm, the muffled screams began to fill the air, having a massive effect on Hatter. He clenched his jaw as his breathing became erratic, and his legs shook. Alice could see that he began to scratch violently at the raised scars on his forearm, causing them to bleed. Without even thinking, she took his hand in hers to stop his attempts at obtaining relief from the mental torment plaguing him. He blushed as he shifted his gaze away from Alice. He never intended for any of them to witness his struggle firsthand.

When they finally approached the enormous building Cat had seen, they witnessed over a dozen women malnourished and trapped in white iron rabbit helmets. A few younger victims dug at the ground, searching for something they would never find. Some older ones lay motionless on the ground, occasionally twitching their limbs. They had given up, but they knew no end would come. Hatter fell to his knees at the sight. Cat moved swiftly to his side and whispered, "No, no. Up. You must stay with us. We're so close."

As they carefully walked in the swarm of iron white rabbits, they noticed that some victims were ensnared in bear traps. The rusty metal had been embedded in their ankles for so long that their flesh began to adhere to it, holding them captive. Some victims snarled as they attempted to scurry away, fearing that the guards had returned to feast. Hatter's breath hitched as he noticed a woman in a trap sitting motionless. Her head hung vacantly to the side, indicating how tired her neck had become from supporting the helmet. Near the mouth of her bear trap was fresh ripped skin from her latest attempt at trying to escape. Her black sundress made her bruised pale flesh seem slightly transparent.

Cat and Alice watched without uttering a word. Alarming the captives was the last thing they wanted to do. Hatter gently laid his scarred hand on her knee and slowly slid her dress up her thigh. She didn't react. On her upper thigh was a large old scar, one that Hatter was very familiar with. He glanced at the others with pure terror, and they rushed to him. "My sweet Rabbit. We're getting you out of here." Hatter whispered, leaning close to her. She lifted her head and held up her hand in response. Hatter placed her hand on this side of his face and kissed her forearm.

7

Without wasting time, Cat knelt by the rusted trap, and Hatter wrapped his arms around Rabbit as tightly as he could without breaking her frail form. Holding his breath, Cat ran his finger along Rabbit's ankle by the embedded teeth. Understanding what was being indicated, she began to sink her fingers into Hatter's biceps. The snapping sounds of the trap harmonize with the blood that burst from the ripping adhered skin around the teeth of the mechanism. Once there was enough space, Hatter slid Rabbit from the trap and into the air. Alice tore off a section of her dress and tightly wrapped it around Rabbit's ankle in a desperate attempt to keep her from losing too much blood.

The white rabbits looked around. While some could scurry away, others frantically ripped at their trapped limbs, desperately seeking freedom. The group rushed into the woods and out of sight as a pig squealed, running from the building with a fuming, plump woman stomping behind it.

"I thought they were a myth. I mean, I know what the rabbit helmets were used for when it comes to the disabling of the Queen's victims, but the rumor of the white rabbits being kept like that I never thought was real!" Cat huffed as they ran through the woods. "Alice, this is where we need you. The carcass of a foul beast is contained within a circle that we cannot access. Because of the location of the carcass, the spell put around it makes it so only outsiders can cross it."

"Okay, one, stop saying carcass. Two, why only outsiders?" Cat laughed and taunted Alice by hissing the word 'carcass' again slowly.

"Outsiders don't make it this far before being devoured. We are used to the rot that has taken over this world. Since we cannot actually die, eating us is a waste. We don't produce the essence to fulfill the guards' feeding desires. The monster's bones are the only material strong enough to break the helmet." Hatter explained, trying his best not to shake Rabbit too much as he ran.

After what seemed like hours, they finally came across a clearing in the woods where grass and flowers started to bloom again. In the middle of the clearing was a large pile of bones nearly twice the size of your average human. Cat gave Alice a nod, and she started walking up to the mound. "Any." She spotted a decent-sized bone not too buried under the rest and removed it. As the pile of bones shifted and settled, Alice darted back to the group.

"How do you want to do this, Hatter?" Alice asked quietly. With a heavy sigh, he shook his head, "Not here. I want to take her somewhere safer. Somewhere that isn't full of rot and death." Cat mentioned a lake not too far away that was untouched by the Queen. He likes to hide there when everything gets to be too much. It's the only place with clean water and life deep in the woods. Alice was happy to go somewhere that did not smell like rotting flesh, even for a short time.

The clearing was gorgeous. A large glistening waterfall cascaded like silver ribbons into the clear lake below. Groups of various types of flowers seemed to dance across the open, lush green field. This was it. This was precisely what Hatter wanted Rabbit to see first. He knew seeing a land as beautiful as this wasn't nearly enough to undo some of the damage done; he also knew her suffering was far from over.

Rabbit flinched and viciously tried to claw her way up Hatter as he sat her in the grass, "It's okay, you're okay. You're safe; it's grass, love." Hatter, Cat, and Alice sat in front of Rabbit. Dread came over the group as they looked at the bone before them. "I don't think I can do this," Hatter muttered, scratching at his arm. "It's going to take all of us," Alice whispered looking at him. "Alice is right, Hatter. One will have to use the bone to pry the two halves apart as the other two pull the halves away."

Hatter finally agreed, knowing that they were right. The pain this would cause Rabbit would be excruciating, and knowing he would be guilty of causing it made him feel ill. The group agreed that Hatter would be towards the front of Rabbit, Cat would pry, and Alice would support the back. "My dear sweet Rabbit. I am so sorry," Hatter whispered a few seconds before Cat started prying at the sides of the helmet.

Rabbit began breathing frantically while she dug her fingers into the ground. The prying motions caused small bubbles of blood to spurt out with a squelching sound, and made Alice want to vomit. Tears streamed down Hatter's face as her whimpering grew louder. Cat sighed heavily, "Honestly, I won't encourage her to slow her breathing. If she passes out, it would probably be for the best. I've barely gotten this mask open a few centimeters."

After ten minutes of sliding the bone up and down the crack of the helmet and prying, Alice let go of the back and moved backward, "I-I need a break. The sounds, I can't." The men looked over at her, fighting not to puke. Cat continued his efforts while Alice lay on the grass looking at the sky. Without a warning, Cat wrapped his hand around Rabbit's throat and squeezed. Hatter's mouth dropped open to protest, but he understood what was happening.

"You know as well as I do this would be better for her if she was unconscious. I would never intentionally hurt a friend, but just enough that she doesn't have to suffer through this whole process," he stated, using his free hand to hold Rabbit's shoulder for support. Once her whimpers stopped, the men laid her on the grass for better leverage. Cat slammed the bone into the crevasse that was created the first time they attempted the removal of the helmet, "Now...we don't have to be as careful breaking the seal. She won't feel it. That said, I'm sure portions of her skin have adhered to the inside, so we need to be careful when pulling the front section off."

Hatter nodded in agreement as he gripped the front part of the helmet. A pop loud enough that it startled Alice rang through the clearing. She sat up just in time to witness Cat discard the bone over his shoulder. Hatter slowly began to lift the front of the helmet from Rabbit's head. Thick strands of purulent discharge formed a vile bridge between Rabbit's face and helmet sections as blood began to trickle towards the grass. "Oh, Gods..." Alice muttered, covering her mouth and laying back down, trying to maintain her composure.

Hatter sat the helmet's front section on the ground next to him as he gently lifted Rabbit off the grass. Cat pulled off the back of the helmet and watched Hatter carry Rabbit to the lake. Tears slowly fell from his eyes as he gently rinsed her face with the cool, clear water. Sections of skin were missing from her jawline and hairline, accompanied by the scars she had obtained during her capture. Cat glanced at Alice with his grotesquely wide smile, "Thank you."

9

Once Rabbit was cleaned up, Hatter lay next to her in the grass, hoping that the sun was enough to keep her warm. Alice watched the couple as she let her mind drift to thoughts of home. This was the first time she allowed herself to think of home since she left. Of course, she had no idea how long she had been in Wonderland, but it had felt like weeks.

"Cat, have you talked to many people who have come here voluntarily?" Alice was plucking blades of grass from the ground in front of her. "Not usually. I tend to stay hidden, but I will approach those forced here depending on their state when I come across them. Rabbit is moving, but don't speak too loudly. She has a lot to process; let Hatter help her." Cat muttered, running his tongue over his teeth. Alice focused on the poor girl lying in the grass ahead of them.

Slowly, Rabbit's eyes fluttered open. Her eyes frantically looked around the sky above her as her breathing quickened. It didn't take long for Hatter to realize she couldn't see. She had been in the helmet so long that her eyes had become accustomed to being in the dark. Hatter covered Rabbit's eyes with a scarred hand without wasting a second, causing her to stop moving instantly. He gently nuzzled her ear with his nose, "You no longer need to fight, my sweet Rabbit. You're safe, and no one will ever take you from me again."

As the group seemed lost in their happy little world, Alice couldn't help but feel an overwhelming dread. Catching the blank stare in Alice's eyes, Cat narrowed his eyes in concern, "Alice..." His tone caught the attention of the others. It was easy for Hatter to realize what Cat was thinking.

All too familiar with the sensation, Alice could feel the viscous, burning bile rushing up the back of her throat. She turned to the side just in time to keep the vomit from projecting towards Hatter. Casually, Cat walked towards Hatter and gave him a nod. "Alice, your time is up." Hatter said softly, "Know that what you are about to experience will end, though it may not feel like it. You will be okay, and when you wake, we won't be here."

She wasn't too sure how to feel about that statement. She didn't want to return home but did not want to stay here. Panic began to set in as she was overcome by the sensation of her stomach being shredded into ribbons.

Tears began to fall as her screams filled the air. The group knew there was nothing that they could do but watch. No words would provide her with comfort, and no actions would ease her coming down.

With no words, Alice writhed in agony in the grass as she watched the flesh melt from her companions' faces and the trees begin to fade. Her skin felt as if millions of fire ants were feasting on it. She began to asphyxiate on the remnants of stomach acid that lingered in her throat. All of her energy was gone, and everything went black.

10

"Yo, Bro!" she heard in a muffled voice as she fought to open her eyes. "Holy shit, babe! We thought we lost you!" Dee stated, assisting Alice as she sat up. Dum grinned at her, "What do you say? One for the road?" Without hesitation, Alice jumped from her seat and ran towards the door, taking care to step over the bodies littering the dance floor. The faint sun seemed to be nothing more than a hallucination. With a deep breath, she headed home.

Perhaps they really are just doing the best that they can. Life could be much worse than it is. Hatter, Rabbit, Cat...I couldn't live the way that they do. No relief, constant terror. Thankfully, I have a place to go, and more or less, I am safe there. Her thoughts drifted between where she was and where she was going. Nothing felt real.

Quietly, she closed the door to the house behind her, trying not to alert her parents to her arrival. They might have passed out somewhere, but she didn't want to risk it.

Glancing at the old family photos on the wall, Alice stopped dead. A picture of her father hung slightly tilted. Alice knew he had struggled with jaundice but she had never noticed his skin's green appearance in the photos.

A few photos over were a photo of her parents, smiling and happy. Being as old as it was, the frame had a crack near her mother's head. Mom had always kept her hair long and covered parts of her face so much that Alice didn't see it odd. In this photo, however, her hair was in an updo. Taking the picture off the wall, she tilted it enough to see under the cracks. Alice's mouth dropped open when she noticed the scars on her mother's face. She dropped the frame, and it shattered on the floor. Glancing at the other photos, she noticed many of her stuffed animals when she was younger were rabbits, and she had always played with silly hats.

Was she really trapped in Wonderland?

Part 2

1

Startled by the sudden knock at the door, Alice's heart raced. Her trembling hands hesitantly turned the doorknob. A man with a wide grin, fiery red hair, and piercing emerald eyes stood on the other side, leaning against the door frame. "Cat," Alice whispered, her voice barely audible. The man's grin vanished, his expression turning grave. "Is your father home?" he asked, his voice low. Alice nodded, her curiosity piqued, and stepped aside to let him in.

Cat took note of the photos Alice had laid out as if she were piecing together a puzzle. "He's upstairs with Mom. They are both currently unavailable, you could say." She started gathering the pictures and hanging them back on the wall. With a nod, he swiftly made his way up the stairs. Inside a room, a man and woman lay on the bed holding hands. With a low growl, Cat sank his nails into the man's thigh, causing him to spring awake.

"Why would you do that?" he whimpered, rubbing his thigh. "She knows who I am. How would she know who I am?" Cat snarled through clenched teeth, "If she knows who I am, she knows who you are, Hatter. We're no longer safe here." Hatter looked around the room, the all-too-familiar feeling of numbness setting in. "What do we do?" he whispered. Cat squeezed the bridge of his nose and shrugged. After a few moments, Hatter reached over and woke the woman beside him, "Rabbit, sweetheart, we have a problem."

She rolled over to face the men and slowly opened her eyes, "Cat?" Nodding in response, Cat sat on the bed, "She knows. I don't know how, but she knows." A wave of terror took over Rabbit as she looked at Hatter. Alice quietly ascended the stairs and stopped in the doorway. The trio looked at her. "What did you take?" Hatter questioned flatly. Alice arched her brow. "Dear Alice, we know you took something. We need to know what you took so we can approach this situation correctly." Cat added, "You're not in trouble in any way; we just need to know what we need to do next."

Alice crossed her arms and looked at the ground. She thought about lying to them, but the situation seemed too severe for games, "Some blue powder called Wonderland. I don't plan on doing it again anytime soon." With a heavy sigh, Hatter placed his head in his hands as Rabbit wrapped her arms around him, desperately trying to provide him with comfort. "Well, that settles it then. That confirms that the twins are here. When night falls, we move." Cat announced as he made his way to the stairs.

Alice and her family spent the rest of the day burning their photos and belongings. None of that mattered anymore. Cat returned as dusk approached. The group gathered in the kitchen for their last meal before fleeing. "I'm sorry for the situation I've put us in. I didn't mean to." Alice whispered, poking at her food. Rabbit reached over and took her hand, "Honestly darling, we knew it would happen eventually." Hatter sat at the head of the table as silent tears fell onto his food.

When they finished eating, they tossed the plates into the fireplace, causing them to smash on impact. Everything needed to burn. Solemnly, Rabbit took Hatter and Alice's hands. With a nod to Cat, they headed out the door. The line of trees near the house, just like everything else, hid a vital secret. Cat led the family to a tunnel at the base of a large tree and ushered them inside. A world Alice had seen before appeared on the other side of the tunnel. "Wait. This is Wonderland." Alice stated in shock as she exited the tunnel. Hatter looked at his daughter without a word and brushed past her.

"Yes. I will explain where we are and what happened later, but we must move and stay as quiet as possible for now." Cat responded, glancing up into the trees. "I'm going to go higher. If the twins have been spotted, I can guarantee the number of guards has increased." Without further warning, he scaled a tree and continued to lead from above.

Bones and dried leaves crunched and snapped under their feet as they walked. Trekking through the carnage that surrounded them didn't bother Alice this time. She scrunched her nose at a section of someone's face dangled from a low-lying section of branches. Rabbit quietly giggled at the reaction as she watched Alice sidestep around the branches. Cat hopped down to a lower section, "Up! Now!" Hatter snatched Alice and hoisted her to Cat before assisting Rabbit into the trees. Once the group helped Hatter into hiding, Cat descended to the floor of the woods below.

Five guards marched towards Cat. Saliva dangled from their mouths as they snarled, dragging a few mutilated bodies behind them. He watched them as they passed, not caring that he even existed. The look of terror embedded on the face of one of the corpses made Cat's blood run cold. This time, things would be more challenging to pull off than last. They hadn't had to run since before Alice was born. Thankfully, since Alice had taken the drug, she was already familiar with her surroundings and what to expect, which saved the group time since there was less to explain.

Looking at her father, Alice noticed his blank expression, and he pushed his face close to the tree. Without a word, she gently rubbed his shoulder. It was evident that at least a portion of what she experienced in Wonderland was true, but just how much she wasn't sure. He shifted his eyes to her and then to Rabbit, who was looking ahead. "Cat, we're stuck." Rabbit called down just loud enough for him to barely hear her.

Curious, Cat joined his friends in the tree and looked ahead. His mouth dropped at the sight. A flock of Jubjubs occupied the trees ahead, ripping the flesh of their victims from the bone, causing limbs and organs to splatter against the ground below. Another group of guards headed in their direction on the other side. "Shit. We'll be here for a minute. Thankfully, since it's dark, we'll be harder to spot." He whispered to the group, "If you want to rest, now is the time to do so. Hatter, you keep tabs on Rabbit. I'll take Alice." Hatter nodded as Rabbit made her way to him.

Swiftly, Cat wrapped his arm around Alice's waist and pulled her onto his lap as he leaned back against the tree. "Sleep." He whispered in her ear, "I won't let you fall. As you can see, your father is in a bad place right now. I don't know how long it will take for him to be okay again, but I feel like you've already done this before." She nodded as she pushed herself closer to Cat's chest. He ran his fingers through her hair, and she desperately tried to sleep.

The screeches from the Jubjubs and the thudding of remains echoed in the night. Cat glanced at the couple periodically as he fought to stay alert. More waves of guards approached underneath, dragging more victims. The Queen wasn't wasting any time. The more bodies she could acquire, the bigger the harvest. The bigger the harvest, the hungrier the guards became. It was an endless cycle of despair.

As dawn approached, Cat looked at Hatter, who was oddly staring at him. Cat quizzically raised an eyebrow. "I just realized where we are." Hatter whispered, "We're by the Bandersnatch." Cat sighed, "That explains that number of guards. The Jubjubs are almost all gone. We'll have to continue in the trees for a bit." They woke the girls and cautiously moved from branch to branch as they progressed. Traversing through the trees, Cat would point out what looked like branches but weren't, "Some of these limbs have been against the trees for so long, they fused with it as the trees grew. Don't step on them. They won't hold our weight."

The smell of petrichor filled the air as dark clouds began to fill the sky. "It rains in Wonderland?" "No, Alice. It doesn't. That smell is because we are approaching Bill's house." Cat corrected as he sped up towards a disheveled shack with smoke billowing from the chimney. Once on the ground, Cat reached up to the group to help them down. "Bill is terrifying, but I promise, stay in line, and he won't hurt you," Hatter warned, running his scarred hands through his hair before knocking on the door.

A tall, lean, bald man opened the door. His head was covered in scars, and his right eye had been sewn shut. "Greetings, Bill. We need passage through the tunnels, please." Hatter stated, trying to sound confident. Bill looked the group up and down as he rubbed his nose on a bloody arm. His hand was covered in rusty nails that had been hammered into the bones, "Payment." "Of course. I will pay." Hatter fumbled over his words, knowing what that meant, "The ladies are not to be touched." Bill nodded and moved aside, letting the group in.

As Bill closed the door behind the group, he pulled a few nails from his hand and proceeded to nail the door shut. They stood there watching Bill grab two large meat hooks and hobble back to everyone, dragging his feet as he did so. Without warning, he grabbed one of Hatter's arms and thrust the hook through the center of his hand. Hatter fell to his knees in pain as blood cascaded down his arm. Both ladies screamed as Cat gently pulled them back behind him. "It's okay. I'm okay." Hatter whimpered just before Bill pushed the second hook through the other hand.

Once satisfied with his work, Bill began to turn the crank that brought Hatter into the air with each loud metallic crank. When he was high enough, Bill kicked a bucket under Hatter and sliced under his ribs, releasing a waterfall of blood to fill up the bucket. Rabbit pressed her face to Cat's back, causing him to gently put his hand on her thigh and pull her closer. Alice watched in terror as her father began to lose consciousness.

"Payment," Bill grunted as he took the bucket of blood and placed it on the table covered in an assortment of various cuts of meat and pulled the pin on the crank.

Hatter's body fell lifelessly to the ground. "Wait. Tunnels at dark." Bill groaned, retreating behind a door that he locked behind him. Rabbit rushed to Hatter and fell to her knees. Gently, she lifted his head onto her lap and stroked his hair. Alice watched in terror as Cat walked to Hatter and ripped his shirt apart, creating bandages. As Cat worked on removing the hooks, the bubbling of blood and squelching sounds made Alice feel sick enough to sit down and cover her face. As soon as night took over the land, Bill returned and opened a section of wall leading to the tunnel, "Welcome."

Rabbit helped tie Hatter onto Cat's back before accessing the tunnels. "I'm sure I will regret asking, but where do these tunnels lead?" Alice squeaked, walking alongside Cat. "Under the castle," Cat responded, grinning at Alice. Alice threw her arms in the air, "Sure. Why not? Why wouldn't they lead under the castle." Cat laughed as Rabbit punched his shoulder, "Whereas it's true, they do go under the castle, they cannot be accessed from the castle. They take us to a clearing that doesn't look like the rest of Wonderland." "Right. Where you and Dad took the iron rabbit helmet off, Mom."

Cat and Rabbit stopped dead in their tracks and looked at Alice. "S-sorry," Alice mumbled, looking at her feet. "How did you know that? You weren't even a thought back then," Rabbit whispered. Alice shrugged, not raising her gaze, "I saw it when I took the drug." Cat looked at Rabbit, who nodded in response, and they continued walking.

As they approached the end, the light from the sun began to illuminate the tunnel. It looked precisely as Alice had seen it. Cat and Rabbit untied Hatter and laid him by the pond. "Is Dad going to die?" Alice whimpered, wiping a tear from her face. Cat started dipping ripped fragments of clothing into the water and handing them to Rabbit so she could clean

Hatter, "Well now, Alice, you seem to know the answer to that already." Alice lay on the grass and stared at the sky. After finishing with Hatter, Rabbit lay next to her daughter and wrapped her arm around her.

"There's no sun. Is there?"

"No, Sweetheart. There's no sun."

"Why does everything I saw when I took Wonderland seem true? How is that even possible if it was a drug?"

"Because, Sweetheart, it's complicated. The twins work for the Queen. They are like her guard dogs. Unfortunately, what they gave you isn't called Wonderland; it's what's known as the Looking Glass. It allows the user to see into the past. I'm sure they told you whatever they thought was needed to get you to take it. That also means the Queen had found us, so we had to run again."

"But Dad is going to be okay?"

"Physically, in time, but every time something happens like this, we get closer to losing him completely to madness. We'll be okay, Alice."

Cat dared not disturb the girls as they fell asleep in the warmth of the light. This was the last time they could sleep soundly; he didn't want to take that from them. Hatter's breathing slowly became less erratic, signifying that his wounds were beginning to heal. Cat stayed close to his injured friend so he wouldn't be alone when he woke up. Noticing blood was seeping from Hatter's mouth, he quickly and carefully turned him on his side, "Easy, Hatter, you can do this."

Violent coughs erupted from Hatter as he began to spew blood and bile across the ground in front of him, causing the girls to wake up. As he started wildly gasping for air, Cat helped Rabbit position Hatter so he was lying on his stomach across her lap. She started rubbing his back as the vomiting subsided. Rabbit gave Alice a weak smile, "Healing causes extreme pain, which is why we long for death and not to be healed." She gave a slight nod in response. A herd of small pesky mome raths scurried over and began lapping at the putrid mix on the ground. "That's disgusting," Alice muttered, gagging.

Hatter weakly tried to push himself off Rabbit's lap, only to collapse against her. Without hesitation, she wrapped her arms around him to keep him from further injuries. "Forgive me, darling." He whispered, fighting to support himself. She nuzzled against his neck, unfazed by the smell. Cat walked over and helped Hatter sit up, "Is the pain

subsiding? Can you use your hands yet?"
"The pain is bearable, and yes, I can use my hands. I feel extremely weak, however. I need more time." Cat nodded at the response and proceeded to walk the perimeter.

"Do you think you'll be able to move by night?" Rabbit whispered, watching Cat. "I have no choice, darling. We must move by night." "Correction, we have to move now!" Cat yelled, running back to the group, "Guards headed this way." Cat and Rabbit heaved Hatter to his feet as Alice rushed to their sides. As quietly as possible, they ducked back into the woods.

The guards' snarls and shuffling echoed behind them as they trudged through the woods. Alice's heart raced. She feared being caught but was more concerned about the broken Hatter being supported before her. This time, knowing these people were her family, the pain and suffering hit differently. Cat slowed to look around. The guards weren't far behind them. The sudden realization that they had gone the wrong way hit like a ton of bricks when they found the farm's fence.

"Oh shit," Alice mumbled, "This is where they keep the White Rabbits." Cat explained they could go around but must watch their step. Various types of traps littered the ground around the gates of the farm. They also knew if they made noise, the captives would scatter. "They don't mean to be so skittish." Rabbit whispered, "We, I mean, they can't see anything or hear well. The Duchess uses the farm to keep the guards happy. Any sounds could mean they were approaching, so they try to run the best way they know how." Hatter's eyes were sorrowful when he looked at her, "You never told me." With a fake smile, Rabbit shook her head, "That's not a burden for you to carry, love." Realizing the guards might have been heading directly towards them, the group continued, silently trying to avoid the traps displayed before them.

The grunting of pigs mixed with the sounds of muffled sobbing of the White Rabbits as some pulled at their chains and ripped at their skin, trying to break free. Tears trailed down Rabbit's face as she forced herself not to look at them. Hatter pulled himself closer to her as they pushed forward.

Once they passed the farm, Jubjubs circled above the trees, screeching and occasionally spilling carnage to the ground below. Alice gagged, causing Cat to chuckle. "I'm so glad you find me humorous, Cat." He shook his head, "It's not that dear. We've dealt with this for so long that I forget some people find it gross. Do keep in mind, this next area is thicker than the woods typically are, so the smell can be a bit overwhelming."

Hatter wiggled, signaling that Cat and Rabbit should let him go. Now that he was able to support himself, they were able to move quickly. "Alice, darling, please walk with your mother in front of me. I can't see behind me."

Hatter instructed softly, leading her to where Rabbit was walking.

The temperature dropped in the darkness that plagued the depth of the woods. Large, deformed turtles were munching on the decaying debris on the ground as they watched the visitors navigate their way. Hatter paused, scanning the dark woods with his eyes. Before he could say anything, a slimy net of silk descended above Alice. Rabbit dove toward her, knocking Alice to the ground. Quicker than it came down, the net ascended in the air. Hatter's mouth dropped open. Two hairy, muscular-looking creatures with eight legs lowered themselves toward Rabbit using the same type of silk as the net.

"What are those?!" Alice shrieked. "Those would be Warblers," Cat responded, scanning the trees, "They produce a vibration that disorients their prey." Tears began to cascade down Hatter's face. "Cat, please." He whimpered. Cat solemnly shook his head slowly, "I can't. I have no way to get close to the net. Your only options, Hatter, are to watch or keep walking." Hatter could no longer see through the tears as he fell to his knees. Rabbit placed her hand over her face, attempting to thwart the headache, "Hatter, my love, you don't want to see this. You and Cat need to guide Alice the rest of the way. Quickly before the guards come."

The warblers used their legs to open a section of netting, allowing them to enter. Rabbit didn't fight back. People rarely escaped one warbler, let alone two. The first unhinged its jaw and placed most of Rabbit's arm in its mouth, serrating it right above the elbow. Flesh ripped, and bones snapped as it pulled back, leaving viscous material dangling in its place. Blood sounded like rain as it kissed the decaying leaves in front of Hatter. Alice ran to the grieving man, "We have to go. It's not safe here." Cat made his way to Hatter and picked the man up as the second warbler sank its fangs into Rabbit's neck, tearing out her throat. Sounds of their mandibles grinding against bones echoed in the shadows as the trio pressed on.

Hatter laid limp against Cat as they made their way deeper into the woods. The wind's chill sent goosebumps across Alice's skin as she helped move branches and debris out of Cat's way. The group wandered into a small, cold, dark opening in the woods. Placing Hatter at the base of a tree, Cat and Alice noticed that he had dissociated. "I thought people don't die here. Cat, I really don't get anything that happens here." Alice admitted sitting next to Hatter and taking his hand. Cat stretched and let out a yawn, "Understandable. No, we don't die. If something happens, causing us to lose limbs, it takes us an incredible amount of time to heal. Because of this, our bodies are usually gathered by the guards and taken to the Bandersnatch. Once there, we are held captive and our essence is harvested for the Queen and her guards. So, we don't die, but we disappear."

Alice raised an eyebrow at Cat, "How do we stop the harvest." Cat stretched out on the ground, laying his head on Hatter's lap, "We stop the Queen. If we can stop the Queen, we can heal the guards. Devouring her heart is the only way to end her reign, and then we can focus on healing the guards and fixing this place. Of course, that's a pipedream." Wrapping her arms around her father's bicep, Alice started thinking about what Cat said. It was possible to save everyone. Cat had fallen asleep. She looked around before exhaustion caused her to give in and drift to sleep.

A wet sensation on her face woke Alice. Rubbing her face, she noticed the silent tears streaming down Hatter's cheeks as he looked at the swarm of Jubjubs circling above them. "We have to go back," he whispered. Cat's eyes shot open, "Absolutely not. I know where this is going, Hatter; it is completely out of the question." Hatter shifted his eyes to Cat, "Is it, though? I'm tired of running. My heart burns, and I want the pain to stop. Either you can walk with me, or I will go alone." Cat turned red with fury as he stomped to his feet. Following his lead, Alice stood and extended her hand to Hatter.

Hatter led the way as the trio started to backtrack through the woods. Looking to his side, Hatter began asking riddles. Alice slowed down and gently took Cat's hand. "Is he talking to himself?" She whispered. "Unfortunately, dear Alice, we have lost him. I beg you, please pay no mind to him right now. There's a good chance he doesn't even know we are here, or where he is for that matter." Hatter continued his way, occasionally laughing, shifting his head from side to side during his conversation.

After performing a small dance, Hatter stopped dead in his tracks. "My hat. Who has my hat?" he said. "I have it, Hatter," Cat announced, knowing very well that he had burned the hat with everything else at the house. "Ah, yes. Thank you!" Hatter resumed walking without even turning around. Alice looked at Cat with tears in her eyes, "He seems so happy."

"He's talking to the children. They were the only thing that made him happy besides your mother after everything happened. Every festival, he made balloon hats for them while repairing hats and taking customer orders. Hatter was one of the only reasons those children still had the ability to laugh."

"So, his mind brought them to him. Can we take him to see them?"

"Dear Alice, those children disappeared a long time ago."

They watched as he carelessly danced through the woods. Alice would wipe away silent tears. Cat squeezed her hand slightly, "Forgive me, Alice. I have no words of comfort to offer." She gave him a slight smile, and Hatter abruptly stopped again. "She's crying.

That sound? What is that sound? It's a clock! Oh, oh yes!" He glanced around as if lost in thought before laughing, "Oh, I have no clock. It's broken. I haven't known the time in quite a while. Do you suppose Rabbit could fix it? We should ask!" He took off running, surprising his companions, who quickly followed suit.

After a while, he slowed back to his normal walking pace, swinging his arms back and forth as he walked, speaking in a playful voice, "But noodles! Oh, I do love noodles. They wiggle and make me giggle, little one." His pace slowed again.

This time, an eerie sense of dread poured from him like a thick fog that hung In the air, "You know, I've always wanted a daughter. When I have one, I hope she's as clever as you. Do you think she would love me? I fear I would cause her shame. I look grotesque; no one would want a father like me. Perhaps she would hide me from her friends. B-But I will try my best; I'm sure it won't be enough, but I will try. Huh? Oh, of course, she would like noodles, silly one! Why is that even a question?"

Alice felt as if someone was squeezing her chest. She fell to her knees as tears cascaded down her face. When she was younger, she would invite friends over to play.

Once her father heard there would be visitors, he would leave for the day. She didn't understand why he would leave, but she never thought it would be because he was ashamed and afraid of how the children would react to him.

Cat wildly brushed away her tears and firmly kissed her forehead, "We're nearly there. Hopefully, when we get there, reality will set back in. I know it's hard." Dragging Alice to her feet, Cat kept her closer as they finished their walk. It didn't take long before the large, rusted door of the Bandersnatch stood before them. Hatter turned around, "How do you suppose we get inside? One doesn't willingly walk into the Bandersnatch."

"That's easy! I can help you get in, but only if you help me. I'm missing a blade of sorts." An old, frail, short man hobbled out of the thicket, "Last I saw it, it was near the marsh. I must have dropped it while collecting mock turtles and oysters for soup. I can show you the way in if you can get it for me. As you see, I'm old and slow these days. Would you please?" With a huff, Cat turned and headed towards the marsh, signaling for the others to follow. Listening to Cat grumble about how complicated everything is in Wonderland, Alice turns her attention to Hatter.

Hatter's chatter had stopped. He seemed to have returned to reality, at least for the moment. Jubjubs circled above, screeching while the ground made a loud squelching sound as the group neared the marsh. Once the blade was in view, Cat laughed abruptly, "Absolutely not. That conniving old man was after the vorpal blade. That blade stays precisely where it is."

"As it should. I did promise you entrance to the Bandersnatch." The old man stood with a guard on each side, "Here are the thieves, guards. Take them away." The man laughed, "Sorry for deceiving you; however, the Queen has announced a bounty on you. I intend to collect that bounty." Hatter glanced around frantically, "The balloons! The children will be so disappointed if I don't bring them!". "Not today, Hatter; the weather is bad, and the children were already told there won't be balloons. They understand," Cat replied dryly, looking at Alice.

As the guards marched closer, Cat wrapped his arm around Alice's waist and whispered, "Do as they say. Do not fight. Let your father stay with the children for now. The Bandersnatch is a special type of hell. It would be wise to listen when I tell you to close your eyes." She nodded as the guards began to grab the trio. The putrid smell of bile and decay flooded Alice's nose, and the guard started to usher her forward. The door popped open with a loud grinding sound when they reached it.

Inside, a large woman resembling a caterpillar snarled as the guards grunted when they walked past. The air was damp, musty, and heavy. The lack of light made it difficult to see. The group was led through a dark hallway lined with doors leading to a larger one at the end of the hall. When they approached, Cat dropped his head and looked at Alice, "Watch the floor, not the walls. Don't look around no matter what you hear." Alice lowered her gaze to her feet when the door opened. The room was brighter than the hallway but smelt twice as bad.

Daring not to raise her head, Alice could see glowing tubes from her peripheral vision. Curiosity got the best of Alice, and she glanced to her left without lifting her head. The wall was lined with bodies anchored to them. One person had tubes protruding from their eye sockets; another had tubes coming from their mouth. Cloudy, viscous material slowly passed through the pipes and into containers on the ground. Alice's body stiffened in response as they walked. Cat chuckled, "Couldn't resist, could you?" She shot him a glare in response as a guard hit him on the back, telling him to stop talking.

Hatter let out a whimper and fell to his knees, causing his companions to look up. Rabbit was attached to the wall ahead of them. Tubes protruded from where each arm was bitten off. Mouths were sewn shut on those who didn't have collection tubes in their mouths to minimize the screams. The guard let go of Cat to assist the guard, trying to hoist Hatter back to his feet. Signaling for Alice to be quiet, Cat vanished into the shadows.

Realizing a prisoner was missing, the third guard let go of Alice as he and the second guard ran back to the front, seeking help from the caterpillar-shaped woman. Cat snuck up behind the first guard and snapped his neck before making himself known again, "Hatter, we have to go." Hatter solemnly shook his head, "No more. I can't run anymore. I-I can't even keep my thoughts in line. I'm not strong enough to continue. Cat, you must guide her now. You know more about this place than anyone else. Please keep my baby safe." Cat nodded, grabbed Alice's hand, and returned to the hallway.

Not far down the hallway, the guards rushed back with the caterpillar lady trailing behind them. Cat shoved Alice behind an essence collector nearby and faded into the shadows. She pressed herself close to the container and squeezed her eyes shut. As soon as shouting erupted from the room that Hatter was in, Cat scooped Alice up and continued to the entrance. The rush of fresh air made Alice dizzy as the pair made their way back into the woods.

"Up." Cat demanded as he held Alice towards a branch above, "Climb up halfway and stop." Doing as she was told, halfway up the tree, Alice sat down and pressed her back to the trunk, breathing heavily. Cat sat beside her and pulled the girl close, "You did fantastic, but we must remain quiet for a while now. It will be extremely busy for a little while. Once they lose interest in finding us, we can keep going. If you want to sleep, you're safe to do so." Unable to ward it off any longer, exhaustion took Alice as Cat kept watch.

5

After a few hours of continuous searching, the guards retreated into the Bandersnatch and sealed the doors tightly behind them. Cat continued to sit quietly, running his fingers through Alice's hair. Knowing what needed to be done made him feel ill. "Dear Alice." He cooed, "We need to go." She lazily sat up and looked at him with a strange look on her face. He arched his brow. "Every time I wake up, I expect to see your face melting away." She whispered.

He shook his head, "Not this time, but from here on, you must do exactly as I say, darling. We need to head back to the farm. The lady who runs the farm is known as the Duchess. I will have to make a trade with her, but she will grant you access to the castle. She absolutely despises the Queen, and with my trade, I know she won't say no. Once inside the castle, the rest is up to you. You have to stop the Queen. For the sake of all of us."

Alice's mouth dropped open, "Why me? There are many better choices." "You are the only one born in Wonderland. It was supposed to be impossible after the Queen took over. So, it falls on you." Cat replied with a grin that was so large it appeared painful.

Hopping down from the tree, he reached up for Alice. With a heavy sigh, she jumped to him. Hand in hand, they continued through the dense woods towards the farm. Being the two of them, it was easier to travel at night. They slipped past a group of guards feeding on the rotting remains of a few unlucky citizens. Cat grinned at Alice, who scrunched her nose as they walked by.

When they were closer to the farm, Cat stopped dead in his tracks and tugged at Alice for her to join him. Signaling for her to remain quiet, he pointed ahead. Five white rabbits scurried around, clawing at trees and digging at the ground. The light from above glistened on the helmets, casting a ghostly halo around each of them. "As horrible as it is to say, they look beautiful." She whispered, watching them. "Indeed. We need to stay quiet so we don't scare them. They have been through enough." Cat replied as they started to walk around where the white rabbits were.

The white rabbits froze and turned in their direction as they passed. They didn't react. It seemed as if they knew they weren't in danger, so they didn't scatter. Cat gave Alice's hand a gentle squeeze as they approached the farm. Hearing the sounds from the farm made Alice feel queasy. "Cat, I was curious: are Rabbit and Hatter in pain in the Bandersnatch?"

"Do you really want that answer?"

"Honestly, I think I already know; I was just hoping I was wrong."

"Remember, their mouths are stitched shut. Your mother did see us, though, so she knows we were there."

"I don't think that makes me feel any better, Cat."

"Well, my sweet girl, this won't either."

Cat reached up and knocked on the door in front of them. A thunderous sound filled the air right before the door opened. "Who dares knock on my door?" an older, short woman boomed. A pig tried to run past, but Cat swiftly scooped it up and handed it back to the woman, "Duchess, do keep an eye on your child, please. Any matter, I come to you with a matter of urgency."

Duchess took a step to the side and waved the pair inside. After closing the door, she drop-kicked the pig into the living room. Alice's mouth dropped open.

"What is this urgent matter, Cat?" she scoffed, waddling over to a chair and sitting down. "I'll cut to the chase. Alice needs access to the castle, and you have the safest way to enter. I come asking for you to allow her to use your entrance."

"How does this benefit me?"

"She's Wonderland born and is going to kill the Queen."

"I like that. What will you give me if I let her use my entrance to the castle?"

"Me."

Alice's head dropped to the side as she gave Cat a blank look. He kept his gaze fixed on Duchess and ignored the reaction. "You?" Duchess questioned. Cat slowly dropped to his knees, "Me. I'm yours to do whatever you wish. I know the type of person you are and the type of place you run, and I will submit myself to you." A huge smile crossed the Duchess' face, "Done." With the snap of her fingers, a large metal collar appeared around Cat's neck. He looked at Alice and gave a nod.

Duchess called after the girl as she opened the passageway to the castle. "It's a straight tunnel. Don't attack at night. Guards stand watch over the Queen as she sleeps. If you're lucky, you'll find one of the other servants. They won't hesitate to help you if guards aren't around. Act fast." With a heavy sigh, Alice entered the tunnel. The heavy door slammed behind her, and she realized she was truly alone now.

The tunnel was littered with. Thoughts of the sacrifices of her family and friends filled her mind. The opening ahead provided some light, and Alice stopped. Tears began to cascade down her face as she fell to her knees. She began sobbing uncontrollably. Fear of failure took over every fiber of her being. "I can't do this alone." She whimpered, clutching her chest. After a few moments, her breathing began to calm, allowing her to stand up and brush herself off. "I have to do this. Failing isn't an option. Everyone gave so much for this opportunity, and I need to make it right."

Lifting her head high, she began prying open the door in front of her.

When the door finally gave way, Alice was shocked to see she was in a garden. Large topiaries were highlighted by beautiful arrangements of flowers with large blooms. Alice swore she could hear them singing as she walked past. Off in the corner, she noticed a group of men acting as a table and two chairs. They were blindfolded, and their mouths stitched shut. Based on how dirty their appearance was, it was obvious they had been there for a while.

The sound of footsteps approaching made Alice jump into a nearby bush and stay as low as possible. Two guards walked past, unaware of the intruder. When they were out of sight, Alice swiftly made her way to the large doors of the castle and crept inside. Massive bookshelves lined the walls of the room she had entered—a fireplace crackled in the middle of one of the walls, entertaining an empty pair of chairs. Noticing there was no place to hide if she needed to, Alice made her way to the opposite end.

Peering around the door, she noticed a large hallway with many windows framed by long, flowing curtains to the left. If necessary, she could hide there. A dozen doors accompanied the windows and a few large wardrobes. Someone could walk out of one of these doors and catch her at any time. On the right was a smaller hallway with a few doors and statues. Directly ahead of her was a large open room with a grand piano and a large staircase on each side of the piano. A few windows and chairs lined the outside of the room, but it felt too risky.

"I need to go up the stairs, but I don't know the castle's layout." Alice thought, "Perhaps I should wait until night. The Duchess said guards watch over the Queen as she sleeps. That would mean they don't roam as much." Quietly closing the door behind her, Alice made her way to one of the wardrobes and looked inside. Little did she know, someone had already noticed her.

Deciding it was too full, she closed the wardrobe and carefully rushed across the hall to open the door. Inside the room was a large, elaborate bathroom. Since it was useless, she closed the door and began walking towards the next door. The hair on the back of her neck rose as she reached for the handle.

Suddenly, a hand wrapped around her mouth pulled her backward across the hall. A few seconds later, Alice found herself in the wardrobe with the door closed. An arm wrapped around her waist and pulled her close as the warm breath of someone closed in on her neck. She squeezed her eyes shut as the sensation of soft lips brushed against the outside of her ear. "Don't move." Their voice was barely audible, "Guards are in a meeting with the knight. It should be over soon; dozens of guards will fill these halls. Wait for them to clear."

The person removed their hand from Alice's mouth and moved it to her shoulder. Gently, they squeezed her shoulder and caressed her collarbone with their thumb, signifying that they were not a threat to her, "Why are you here?". "I'm house hunting." Alice teased. They rested their head against hers, "Very funny. I need to know. Why are you here?" "I'm going to kill the Queen." She sighed. Their body tensed up, "Really? By the Gods, please tell me you aren't joking with me. Are you really going to free us?" Alice gave a silent nod as the door ahead opened.

Guards flooded into the hallway, followed by the knight. The embrace tightened around her. The guards returned to their post.

"When I open the door, we will go directly into the meeting room across the hall. Do not stop until you are inside." Alice nodded as they reached forward and opened the door. Without daring to look behind her, she rushed over and threw open the door to the room. Once inside, she dove under the table in the center of the room.

Hearing the door lock didn't comfort her. The person with her pulled out a chair and sat down. She looked over at the black slacks and shiny black shoes. "You have no reason to hide. If I wanted to hurt you, I would have done so already." A man's voice cooed, "I want to help you as much as I can." Alice cautiously crawled out from under the table and stood up.

To her surprise, the King was sitting at the table. His head was propped on a freshly bandaged hand. His shoulder-length black hair highlighted the bruising on his face and neck. She slowly walked over to him and, without thinking, wiped away the blood that was running down his cheek from his broken cheekbone, "You're bleeding." He pressed his face into her hand, "That's normal, but not why we're here. She's inaccessible at night. I can provide you with safety until morning. I will purposely make her mad at that time to keep her attention while you strike."

"How can you provide me with safety? Not to be rude, but you don't quite stand up for yourself."

"I don't because there is no point. She doesn't injure me enough to have me sent to the Bandersnatch, but she has caused me to pass out for multiple days because I spoke against her. It isn't that I don't stand up for myself; I don't have the energy anymore. If I don't argue, it's not as bad. We have separate rooms. I can hide you in mine for the night. However, to do so, you must make me a promise."

"What promise is that?"

"No matter what happens, no matter what you hear, don't look. I'm covered in scars and bruises. Tonight will likely bring more, but I don't want you to witness it. I will hide you in a vent, but please keep your back to my room."

With a heavy heart, Alice agreed. The King grabbed a pen and napkin from the table and began drawing Alice a map of where she needed to go. He placed an 'X' where guards were stationed along the way. Reaching into his vest pocket, he pulled out a shirt, "Wear this. It will help to mask your scent from the guards. Be safe, and come to me around dusk."

With a weak smile, he reached forward and ran his fingers through Alice's hair. Taking a chance, he pulled her towards him. She didn't resist as he gently pulled her into his lap and wrapped his arms around her. Softly, he nuzzled her ear with his nose, "Please, just for a moment." Understanding that he needed comfort, Alice shifted her weight and returned the embrace of the broken King, "It will be over soon."

7

The King released Alice and slipped out the room. After putting on the shirt the King had handed her, Alice looked over the map. "What would Cat do if he was me? I need to sneak up two different sets of stairs in the daytime without making noise," Alice muttered to herself. She folded the map and tucked it into her bra strap. Walking to the door, she stopped and kicked off her boots. After making sure no one was in the hallway, she dashed over and hid her boots in the wardrobe.

Now that her scent had been hidden and her steps were quiet, she returned to the large room with the piano. Taking a deep breath, she dove under the piano and looked around. According to the map, no guards were on duty between this staircase and the one at the end of the room upstairs. Crawling from under the piano, Alice quietly ascended the stairs. As she reached for the handle, she heard a voice speaking on the other side.

Slowly, she opened the door a crack and saw the King speaking with a few guards, "The

Queen changed her mind and demanded her wine in the garden. I need you to go to the kitchen and gather her wine and glass. I heard there was quite a commotion outside of the gates. Please address this after you are done setting up for her." Alice watched as the guards grunted and shuffled away.

He turned towards the door and nodded at Alice, "War room is empty. Use the vent to get to the next staircase; keep right." As he turned and left the room, Alice darted down the hall and to the war room. Inside was a board covered in photos that had been scribbled out. She decided it was best not to inspect it further and headed to the vent. Once it was opened, she noticed pieces of a skeleton tucked inside. Climbing over it, she reattached the vent cover and crawled to the right, as the King said.

As she crawled through the walls of the rooms, she got a glimpse of the horrors within. One room had a decaying corpse still attached to a rack. They had been stretched so far that the only thing attaching the top half to the bottom was the strings of entrails between the two. Shaking her head, she continued forward. The next room contained a woman attached to a Judas Cradle, crying.

Deciding that looking into the rooms was a bad idea, Alice shifted her gaze to the bottom of the vent and continued to the end of the tunnel. She could see the final staircase ahead of her. High heels echoed in the room just as she reached the vent cover. Sliding backward, she lowered her body closer to the ground.

The King walked up to meet the Queen. "My wine isn't in the garden, " she hissed, grabbing his throat and sinking her nails into the bruised flesh, "I told you to have it ready for me, and yet I'm still waiting." "I'm very sorry. I sent the guards to do it a while ago. I will take care of it myself, Your Majesty." The Queen tossed the King to the floor and spat on him as she walked away.

Rolling onto his back, he glanced at Alice in the vent and waved her out. Quietly, she made her way to the King. "I cleared everyone out in your way. Make your way to my room quickly before the guards return." He whispered, pushing himself to his feet. With a nod, Alice darted up the stairs and through the door.

Just as promised, the hallway was empty. Not taking any chances, she went inside the room marked on the map and went inside. Looking around, she started to think she had the wrong room. A few pillows and a blanket lay on the floor in the corner of the room. The blood-stained dresser housed a shattered mirror.

Trusting in the map, she opened the vent cover. Inside the vent was a small box. Once safely tucked inside the vent, Alice turned her attention to the box. She slowly opened it. Her heart sank as she saw the photos inside. Flipping through them, confirmed she was in the right room. The photos in the box were of the King smiling with a beautiful woman and of them at various events with townsfolk. After carefully placing the photos back in the box, Alice laid down to rest.

As dusk approached, the King returned to his room. A smile crossed his face when he knelt near the vent and noticed Alice sleeping inside, "Sweetheart, I just wanted to let you know I'm here. You need to scoot back just a bit more. I will keep the lights low to help hide you." Alice slowly lifted her head and pushed herself backward.

Meeting his gaze, Alice pointed to the box, "Who is she?" The King sighed, "Those are pictures of my beloved Queen and I. They are all I have left of her now, and if her sister saw I still had them, I-I don't know what would happen." She said nothing more as she watched him stand and dim the lights, "Remember my request. Nighttime doesn't treat me well; please don't watch." He walked to the corner, lay on his pillow, and covered up.

As previously requested, Alice turned her back towards the room. Gently taking the box, she held it in front of her, keeping it hidden. This way, the box wouldn't be seen and taken away from the King if she was caught.

It didn't take long before the door was thrown open. The King didn't move. The Queen walked into the room in her nightgown and crossed her arms. The knight was close behind her, "Wake up, you piece of shit. My knight is feeling…lonely." " Please, not tonight. My body hurts," The King whimpered, sitting up and facing them. "Just imagine how much worse it will feel when you two are done playing." Turning to the knight, she laughed, "Remember, he has no authority to tell you no. Return to your room when you finish, and make sure his room is locked." The Queen slammed the door behind her, and the knight began to remove his clothes.

Alice's eyes grew wide once she realized what was going on. She could do nothing to help without putting him more at risk. She covered her ears to drown out the King's whimpers as she silently cried. Once the knight locked the door, Alice barreled out of the vent. The King was curled up into a ball in the corner of the room.

Being careful to avoid the blood on the floor, she tip-toed over to the broken man. Gently, she picked up his blanket and covered his bruised and bleeding body with it. "I'm okay," he whispered through his tears, "This was nothing compared to what normally happens. I appreciate your concern." She sat beside him, running her fingers through his hair until he fell asleep, then returned to the vent. Hatred for the Queen raged inside of her.

When morning came, the King tapped on the vent. "The Queen will be here to let me out soon," he whispered, sliding a blade he stole from the kitchen into the vent. "Through the throat is enough to disable her for a few minutes so we can finish the job." She silently took the blade and held it, ready to attack. The King set the cover to the vent against the entrance without closing it, allowing Alice to attack faster.

Using a bucket with a mixture of blood and water in it, he grabbed a shirt and began cleaning the mess from the night before off the floor. The King didn't look up as the door unlocked and was pushed open. The knight stood in the doorway, "Your presence is requested in the banquet hall." "No." the King replied, not looking up. The knight wasted no time turning around and walking away. "Be ready. When it's reported that I said no, she will storm in here faster than you would expect." He stated flatly. Alice gripped the blade's hilt tightly as the thunderous roar of the Queen stomping filled the air.

She burst in through the open door. "What do you mean, no?" she screamed. Slowing her pace, she walked over to the King, who sat up on his knees and looked at her. "I refuse," he replied. The Queen raised a balled fist, causing the King to close his eyes. As the fist came down with rage, it suddenly stopped. When he opened his eyes, he saw the blade protruding through the center of the Queen's neck.

Alice stepped back and let the Queen's body fall to the ground. Without hesitating, the King crawled over and removed the blade. Furiously, he slashed open her shirt and began carving through the cartilage of the Queen's ribcage. When he had enough cut open, he reached in and snapped the ribs protecting her heart. Alice scrunched her nose as she watched the King retrieve the heart.

9

The King held the heart in his hand and stood up. The blood of his abuser flowed freely down his arm. "Come, Alice," He commanded, walking out of the room. The guards stopped, stared at the sight, and the pair walked past. They didn't try to attack but followed them obediently.

Once they made their way to the balcony overlooking the town, the King held the heart up high. The townsfolk and guards all turned to watch the spectacle before them. The King handed the heart to Alice, "Tell the heart you are the Queen and take a bite to seal the deal." Taking the heart in her hands, Alice brought it to her lips and whispered. When she was done, she sank her teeth into the meatiest part of the organ, causing blood to spill from her mouth and to the floor.

"All hail the new Queen!" The King exclaimed. The guards fell lifelessly to the ground. Alice shook her head, "Not quite your majesty. I don't want to be Queen." He lowered his gaze towards his feet. "I can't do this alone.

I need a Queen," He muttered solemnly. "I would love to be your Queen if you'll have me," A soft voice responded from behind Alice. The King's mouth dropped when he noticed the former Queen standing behind Alice. "I know how loved she was. I told the heart I wanted her to return to her role as Queen."

The Queen walked over to the King and took his hand. Gently placing his hand on the back of her head, he gently kissed her. "The Queen of Hearts reign of terror has officially ended. All Hail the Red Queen!" The King shouted, holding the Queen's hand in the air. Slowly, the guards rose one at a time and saluted the royals. "That wasn't the only thing I requested from the heart. I asked that Wonderland be returned to how it was during the Red Queen's reign. It might take some time, but hopefully, the land will recover. The guards seem to have reverted already."

In the distance, Alice noticed Cat smiling at her. Next to him stood Duchess, holding a young child in her arms. "Alice, as savior of Wonderland, what can we give you as a token of gratitude?" The Queen asked, wrapping her arm around Alice's. "I just want to go home. I want to be able to live with my parents and actually be happy," Her voice cracked as she responded.

"You are absolutely free to do so," The Queen gestured off to the side where Rabbit and Hatter stood hand in hand, smiling at their daughter. "Oh, and Alice." The Queen added, "The White Rabbits are free." Waving goodbye to the royal couple, Alice made her way through the crowd and threw her arms around her parents. Hand in hand, they left the courtyard and started back towards their town.

When they arrived, they were shocked to see their house as if they had never burned anything. The townsfolk smiled and waved at the cars that now drove on the streets. Alice was free to return to a life she never knew—one where her family was finally safe and happy.